Daniele Mencarelli is a poet and author. Born in Rome in 1974, he now lives in Ariccia, Italy. He is a regular contributor to several Italian newspapers and magazines. *Everything Calls for Salvation*, his second novel, won the 2020 Youth Strega Prize.

Octavian MacEwen is a translator based in Britain. He studied Italian at the universities of Edinburgh and Bologna, and holds a Master's Degree in Translation Studies from Durham University.

THE HOUSE OF GAZES

Daniele Mencarelli

THE HOUSE
OF GAZES

*Translated from the Italian
by Octavian MacEwen*

Europa
editions

Europa Editions
27 Union Square West, Suite 302
New York NY 10003
www.europaeditions.com
info@europaeditions.com

Copyright © 2018 Mondadori Libri S.p.A., Milano
First Publication 2023 by Europa Editions

Translation by Octavian MacEwen
Original title: *La casa degli sguardi*
Translation copyright © 2023 by Europa Editions

*This work has been translated with support from
the Italian Ministry of Culture's Centro per il libro e la lettura.*

Library of Congress Cataloging in Publication Data is available
ISBN 978-1-60945-972-7

Mencarelli, Daniele
The House of Gazes

Art direction by Emanuele Ragnisco
instagram.com/emanueleragnisco

Cover design and illustration by Ginevra Rapisardi

Prepress by Grafica Punto Print – Rome

Printed in Canada

CONTENTS

For strugglers

THE HOUSE OF GAZES

THE TOWN

1

I t's not an awakening. It's a jolt.

Every morning I find myself prostrate in bed, gasping for breath, my heart racing, my body trembling, a frenzy of movement.

"I remember nothing." That's what I repeat to myself every morning.

"Remember nothing." That's my goal for the evening.

I get up jerkily, an automaton with no coordination or coordinates. My trousers are full of piss. I stretch my foot out to brush aside the pot my mother leaves next to the bed. Empty, as usual.

It's six in the morning. I'm breathing like I've just surfaced from a black ocean, soundless and dreamless.

She's there, asleep on the three steps leading to my room. Only despair can send you to sleep on three steps. My mother is a hapless dowser; her water is the three children she cares for, but one, the last, came out of her with an invisible disease affecting his brain, or heart, or all the blood flowing through his body.

My mother rears up in restless pain, one arm numb, posed like a contortionist at the end of a show. She looks at me like she's hoping for something, a change that isn't coming.

I'll end up forgetting her too, no longer loving anything because I can't defend anything, I can't save anything. So, destroy the world, end it all. I don't want to survive my mother, my father, everything that'll burn into nothingness.

A succession of expensive doctors found no solution besides

medication and hourly care, besides giving different names to what I supposedly do or don't have. Manic depressive. Borderline. Personality disorder. Generalized anxiety disorder. And other names that forgetfulness has snatched away.

But I'm not sick. I'm immeasurably alive, like a beast more conscious than other beasts. People are no longer allowed to wonder, to fully embrace the senselessness on which we've based absurd certainties. Because life, work, and raising a family are things you have to believe in, just as a soldier must believe in war. Yet it only takes the smallest thing to set fate in motion, to put an end to it all. Because everything ends, nothing remains. It's nothingness that kills me, that's led me to this empty present. I should just stop asking, searching. I should just pretend not to notice the absence, everywhere, of something, someone.

An endless absence that makes even love unhappy.

So many people tell me to write, to throw everything into it.

Because I write poetry. A couple of years ago I made my first appearance in a literary magazine, then more followed. A lot of people think highly of me, even important poets.

But poetry bears witness to pain, it doesn't cure it. Words have always accompanied me. They're crystal and root, journey and blade. They're everything but medicine. Poetry doesn't cure. If anything, it opens, unstitches, uncovers. But I no longer have the strength to create poetry.

I look at the image before me in the mirror, my chest covered in burns from cigarettes that dropped from my mouth in my sleep, a bruise on my forehead from God knows what. I'm twenty-five years old; all that remains from the last four is this image in the mirror. Plus, the weeping pain and everything hammered into the heart of a father and mother, a brother and sister, the lives interrupted by my fall, as precise as an Olympian's dive.

I've managed to sweep away four years. Step by step, I'll sweep everything away.

I t's more a destiny than a disease. A hateful oddity. What enriches others is a source of pain for me. It's the fate of those born to succumb.

While others smile at nostalgia, I weep. Memory is a poison I can't measure out. It's been burning me since I was a little boy who wanted to go back, back to the time of a happiness as remote as a childhood I never lived.

While others benefit from love, given and received, I suffer. Something incomprehensible happens in me that makes me perpetually experience love on the threshold of farewell. I don't accept that what I love can leave me, that there's a time within which to live and die. My loves are as deep as the universe, and no one must touch them. But that's not how it is.

People stop living as if it were natural. They resign themselves to death and give up.

My loves die every day. It's fear that swirls the images in my head. That's where cruel scenes play out, where my loves end in tragedy, and I suffer as though these visions were flesh and blood.

Fear is my demon. It turns everything into a disaster written before it's lived. With fear, I've lost before I've even fought.

So, treat it.

Swallow the medicine that makes you forget, that kills fear.

And I've tried every medicine, right down to this last one.

Now I go out to drink, and I drink to go out.

On the form for the last admission, the doctor wrote: "Alcohol abuse as a fallback from drug addiction."

A fallback will kill me, the last card in the deck.

A typical day involves looking for my car as a first step towards forgetting again. It often takes hours. Remembering the night before is like trying to recall the months before birth. A void that occasionally spits out a color, a nightmare, a face emerging from God knows where.

I find it with a broken window and its grill folded in on itself. I had three accidents yesterday, the last at two in the afternoon after dozing off at the wheel. I remember this perfectly. Forgetfulness progresses as the hours go by, starting in the late afternoon.

I remember nothing about the accident a month ago, only finding myself upside down in the middle of the road, woken by cars screeching to a halt, instantly sober, at least for the first five minutes.

Ever since that accident, my father has stopped repairing my car. The mechanics where he takes it are all his friends and he doesn't want me seen "in my state."

The last time a friend of his gave me a coffee, I was trembling so much I couldn't even get it near my mouth. My father made me drink it, holding the plastic cup up to my mouth like I was a paralytic, trying to downplay the situation to his friend.

I've never seen him put on such a bad performance.

The first thing I drink is all that counts. What comes next doesn't matter.

What matters are the stations on my journey: two bars, one at the beginning of town and one at the end. Never mind which is the start and which is the finish.

A glass of white at each bar. A glass of white from beginning to end. It's the cheapest thing on offer.

The journey's destination is unknown. The tremors aren't. They come like quakes, ever stronger.

But today something new seems to be paying me a visit.

The shaking has cramped me up and bent my head. I can't hold it up anymore.

Perhaps it's the advancing delirium, or maybe I'm finally dying.

I go towards the hospital, then forgetfulness knocks, and I open.

I wake up to find myself on a stretcher with an IV in my arm, my wrists bound with tape, my father and mother, summoned back to their role, on one side, two policemen on the other. Feeling constricted by the tape makes me instantly lose my cool. Release me. Right now. But that's not what happens.

A very young doctor stares at me from a distance like she's watching a dragon.

A firmer tug and the tape snaps. I pull out the IV and blood starts gushing out of my vein in long spurts. I see people running to avoid being baptized by my blood, even the policemen.

They discharge me out of pure exhaustion. It would be the third hospitalization in two months and the psychiatrist on duty—the woman who was looking at me in horror—said I wasn't "medically treatable." Shameful words burst out of my mouth towards her.

I'd like to know what words I used, but that's in the realm of forgetfulness.

We get home. My father says nothing and looks at nothing, going to his room with slumped shoulders. I've never seen him so small, a man the size of a mountain, strong enough to bend iron.

My mother stays beside me, suddenly taking my hand, beckoning me to follow her out into the night.

"If it has to happen, let's at least do it together."

My mother takes me to the colossal bridge that leads into my town, stopping right in the middle.

"So, we can finally stop suffering."

My mother is a feather ready to fly. She's there on the brink of life and feels nothing. She longs for the death I've been giving her drop by drop for four years. I'm killing those I wish to protect from any natural event. The evil is me. I'm the one destroying everything.

We stay there for a time that isn't seconds and minutes. The thought crosses my mind of flying down two hundred feet in an angel's flight with my mother. All it takes is to transform this thought into a nervous impulse and everything will be over. I'm about to do it, and my mother with me.

Instead, I take her hand and lead her home. She no longer seems present. Her eyes possess the weariness of someone who has ceased to live, even though we're returning from the bridge on our own two feet.

I get into bed almost lucid. This hasn't happened for as long as I can remember. In place of sleep, I have tremors, a beating heart deep inside my ears. I hear footsteps on the three steps. She's bringing me a sleeping pill, taking off my blood-stained sweater, still daring to caress me. She goes to sit on her step, an exhausted sentry, a pile of flesh and bones. I turn away, no longer knowing what to wish for.

When I call Davide, I'm not ashamed. If you ask for help, you have to do it properly. I can't afford shame.

Davide is a poet, a friend, my only friend. He's the editor of a literary magazine, the one I debuted in a couple of years ago. I rely on him, partly because I've no one else. I have to break the chain I've wrapped around my waist, around my whole body. I don't know what I want to become, what to be, but I have to try to stay alive.

It's a short phone call. Davide knows the maelstrom I'm in. He tells me he'll get to work, without dwelling too much on what and where. The important thing is I get out of the house.

Anyway, what objections can I raise? What job—in my sorry state—can I possibly aspire to? I don't need to look over my shoulder to see all the failures I've amassed in recent years. A thousand study courses taken up and dropped, as many jobs. I've been an air-conditioning salesman, a temporary traffic warden, a bookbinder, a kitchenhand. I studied Law for two years, then Communication, dropping both without much regret.

Until the age of twenty, I managed to keep the gaze at bay. Then it all blew up. My nerves cracked under the constant stress; friends and drugs came to the rescue. A fun despair, at least at first. But as the group realized that my pleasure concealed a homicidal intent, complete loneliness set in. Christ, you do drugs or drink for fun, at most you die from something random like a car crash, but with a certain restraint, a yardstick, a capacity for management. If you go beyond that limit, if instead of unbridled joy you start producing suffering, then you instantly become an outcast.

A nuisance to even pass in the street.

Davide calls me back in the evening. A friend of a friend. A service cooperative.

I'll be a janitor, cleaning and portering.

When he tells me where I'll be working, I don't give it much thought. I write everything down on a sheet of paper.

For years now, dinner has become a procession of glances and silences. We eat to feed our bodies, no longer to create a ritual of family sharing, dialogue, and play. It wasn't always this way. Then I came along. The thought takes away what little appetite I have. I just want to throw myself on the ground and kiss the feet of those I love, those I'm hurting. I just want to say sorry, to be able to go back, not to be endowed with what I am.

"Davide has found me a job as a janitor at Bambino Gesù hospital."

My mother and father fix their eyes on me. From what I can tell, they have different feelings. They've greeted the news in silence.

My mother is afraid. I can read it on her lips. "They treat children at Bambino Gesù. You were there as a child."

Perhaps because of the memory, perhaps for some other reason, my mother starts to cry.

"It's no place for you, seeing sick children. Are you sure?"

I don't answer. I look at my father, sensing he wants to say something too. In the end, he stays silent. He barely speaks at the table anymore, let alone looks me in the face.

That evening, we make a deal. I tell them I won't go out as long as I can drink in peace at home. My parents eventually agree, provided it's just the little alcohol needed to bring up everything coursing through my body.

Forgetfulness comes early. The last image in my memory is of my mother. I see her the same way as ever, a spinning top around my bed, less talkative than usual. The news about Bambino Gesù is ceaselessly brewing within her. I read it in her every gesture, in the sudden pauses she permits herself, overcome by thoughts.

Throughout the journey, I try to remember the last time I had a sober dialogue with another living being. Nothing comes to mind. Now fear is mounting, one mile at a time. Drugs and alcohol have turned the shyness of the little boy I once was into something else: filthy shame. One by one, I feel all the gazes of mankind on my back. Those gazes undress me, bring me to my knees, continually pass merciless judgement on my state. Social phobia, another disorder to put on my CV. I only defeat it with alcohol, but this morning I can't drink. They'd notice. Now I go from sober to wrecked with half a glass of wine.

I take the Appian Way towards Rome, finishing off what little remains of my fingernails. I could've had an anxiolytic, but it's too late.

After the Lungotevere, I go up to the Janiculum. I haven't been up here for years. A New Year's Eve ages ago, I can't have been even eighteen. Further back, a grainy memory. The cannon firing at the stroke of noon, the puppet theatre, me holding hands with my mother and father. Here it is. Nostalgia arrives like a boulder flung from afar, but luckily there's no time: a toothless unlicensed parking attendant offers me a contemptible spot, practically on a bend. Alright then. It's ten to ten and I've never arrived late in my life. This is what my insecurity demands.

If you arrive, you arrive early, even hours ahead.

Before passing through the gate, I look across from the viewing area just ahead, towards Rome stretched out to its farthest limits, the buildings directly below Regina Coeli prison, not far from the enormous white Tomb of the Unknown Soldier. Beauty lavished unsparingly. Higher up—towering over everything—is Monte Cavo, the Castelli Romani. My home.

The hospital is divided into blocks. I ask a security guard where the service cooperative office is. He starts to show me the way and I immediately panic.

Ever since my social phobia erupted, I can't make eye contact with people. I look away. God knows how I appear to observers. I ask myself this question all the time. The answers are always the same: a lunatic, a drug addict, a poor simpleton, often all three at once. Only forgetfulness removes this question and the answers that follow from my mind.

I set off thinking of the first direction in the endless sequence given to me by the security guard. I have to pass through an underground passageway—a very long corridor connecting the various pavilions—on the first basement floor.

At first sight, this endless tunnel reminds me of a long artery joining organ after organ, perhaps because of the red brick floor and lower section of the walls. I make at least ten wrong turns down here, encountering doctors, nurses, empty stretchers. Finally, I reach the cooperative office. It's next to the medical records archive.

Anxiety explodes when I see at least seven or eight people sitting around in grey uniforms. The women are wearing scrubs in the same color; the only contrasting element is a yellow collar. I try to smile at everyone, but I don't look anyone in the face. I sweat, straining to control my breathing, to give it a regular, calm cadence, though I'm well-aware it's in vain.

My future colleagues shake my hand, introducing themselves. I forget their names the moment I hear them.

"You must be the new guy."

A man in his forties comes towards me. He's the only one

without a uniform, the only one I look in the eye. He extends his hand without any sign of welcome.

"I'm Fabio, the foreman."

I shake his hand. "Daniele."

"Know how to use a scrubber-dryer?"

I've never heard this composite name before. I shake my head and he smiles at the other workers. My state often confuses the real and unreal, but in this case it's not social phobia that mixes up what's real and what's in my head. Fabio smiled at the others as if to say, "Get it?" or "Hear that?" Embarrassment slaps me in the face.

"Ah! The guy with connections is here!"

The comment—in a man's voice—resounded behind me. I turn around and see other faces added to the audience. Now they're all looking at me. I can't tell who made this remark.

"Can you at least clean a window?"

I instinctively nod. I know how to clean a window, for Christ's sake. Fabio responds by diving into the office. I hear him rummaging; he comes back with a wiper for cleaning windows. I've seen desperate people wielding that contraption at traffic lights. When he hands it to me, I try to remember their movements, then I perform like a mime on an invisible window.

Everyone laughs.

I'd give anything to hurl myself at Fabio, to headbutt that lovely smile, then—one by one, women included—to beat the shit out of all the others. Or simply to escape from there.

"Come on then, you have to sign the contract."

I enter the little office. All around are jerry cans full of detergent, mops, huge rolls of rubbish bags. Fabio hands me the contract.

I sign. It's March 3 1999.

"You start tomorrow morning at six. Management has put you on the external team. It's the position where you earn the most because of the night shifts. At least four guys at this hospital have been waiting ages to move to that position. If you noticed some stares before, now you know why."

I nod. I can't help but smile to myself. A guy with connections gets hired as a company manager, not as a cleaner in a hospital.

Fabio goes back to reading pay slips. He doesn't even look at me. Seeing there's no one outside, I breathe a sigh of relief.

Instead of retracing my steps along the underground walkway, I step out into the open. I realize I'm standing beside the other entrance, the one to the ER. It's marked with a huge sign, ED, EMERGENCY DEPARTMENT. As though conjured by my mind, a siren rings out. The electric barrier quickly rises and the ambulance rushes in at full speed. I stand still, following a security guard's instruction to everyone around. From inside the cabin, mingling with the roar of the siren, a child's cries are clearly audible. Loud cries, linked to God knows what pain. The ambulance stops in front of the ER. I walk in the opposite direction, still dazed by the siren and cries.

The hospital is carefully maintained down to the last detail. Every few feet, imperative signs recall the smoking ban, even outdoors, and I'm on two and a half packs of cigarettes a day. MS, the 'hard' variety. The people I encounter give the impression of having a specific goal, a place waiting for them. Everything is order, cleanliness, and precision, at least that's how it appears at first sight. It's not like the other hospitals I've been to lately, especially the one in Albano, a building that's seemingly survived a bombing, both inside and out: if a place's beauty even remotely represents its spirit, no wonder you die so easily in there.

The parking guy wants another thousand liras; I give him five hundred.

The idea that from six tomorrow morning I'll have to live with these pricks stresses the hell out of me. Who knows if I can handle it. I consider my mother's words for a moment. I could always say the hospital environment wasn't for me, given my sensitivity. It makes me laugh a little, me exploiting the thing I hate most in the world. Sensitivity. The fool's yardstick. As though every other human feeling can somehow be measured. Hang the sensitive poet's rhetoric. Speak, if anything, of fragility, of beings born with the thinnest skin, an extremely low number of antibodies against every good and evil in the world, from pain to tenderness, as well as melancholy and love. People you can pin with next to nothing. It just takes a flower to pierce their skin.

I drive homeward, leaving Rome behind—at least almost all of it—until I reach a bar in the Piramide area. The free parking space right in front feels like an invitation from an invisible friend.

"A glass of white."

It's one of those days that heralds spring, an arrival announced not by visible signs, but the slant of the light, something ineffable, untranslatable.

Alcohol is a wave of softness, sweeping away the sharp edges that wound me.

At least until forgetfulness, I can speak naturally, laugh just as naturally, hug. With alcohol, I'm mild, fun, great company in short.

Aside from the cost issue, alcohol is the ultimate drug. Perhaps that's why it earned legality. Maybe, without anyone knowing, they carried out selections in high places before making it legal, a kind of competition between all psychotropic substances in which the prize was legality, the state's guarantee, the perfection of perfections. I came to alcohol the day I promised the world I'd give up the illegal drugs that were destroying me, not to mention the money I was burning that wasn't mine, the danger of arrest, everything that can happen to people who associate with all kinds of criminals. I began taking drugs when I was seventeen. In those days, it was a game for a young guy in a young crowd, and for a while it carried on like that, from a light-hearted drink to a Saturday night ending at Sunday lunchtime. Back then, smoking, pills, ecstasy, raves around town, and clubs all did the trick. I can't say which came first, what the order of the sums was. The thing I didn't calculate at the time was my mental and psychological state. Lighting a match in the middle of a meadow is one thing; lighting one inside a gas-filled room is another altogether. Everyone switched to cocaine at pretty much the same time due to the consensus that—when it came to drawbacks and dangers—there was no comparison between a synthetic drug, created in some Dutch laboratory, and a "natural" drug. Also, because pills impaled a fair number of friends on the day of their end, which didn't always coincide with their death. Some arrested, some "damaged," their brains fried by chemistry. Others actually dead, confused with guard rail, burned.

What I loved about cocaine was the feeling of control, unknown and always longed for. It may sound absurd, but it affected me like a sleepless sedative, capable of laying reality at my feet. Nothing uncontrolled could happen, and even if it did, I could command it. But for eighty thousand liras a gram. And while alcohol has its climax—sought and achieved—cocaine doesn't, like every other narcotic, so you inevitably return to the starting point, in a comedown of nerves and yearning, with a ferocious urge to find more, then even more. Cocaine led to the split from the group, from all my friends. I didn't want to deal with myself and I couldn't. Besides, at this point my sickness was obvious, along with my exaggerated behavior and reactions. You try going out with a guy who's deeply moved by a song or who—incited by the most absurd paranoia—argues to the point of slapping someone. The only ones left around me were trusted dealers and cocaine addicts I met on the street, people of every type, age, and curse.

But since neither I, nor my parents had any capital that I could burn through—as was the case for so many—the cracks soon emerged. Three hundred thousand liras vanished, the First Communion gold stashed away somewhere, sudden debts, sudden university fees. It was my brother who became convinced I had a problem. Some acquaintances told him. The limitation of provincial life. What little world was still standing collapsed in the eyes of my mother and father, who had survived up to that point because it takes time and dedication to destroy a parent's trust in a child. That transition decreed its end until further notice. I promised to overcome it, sincerely. I experienced the chain of addiction; when I felt I'd succeeded, I raised my glass for a toast.

A celebration of the new slavery.

"You've been drinking."

My mother no longer needs to see my face or hear me speak. All it takes is for me to set one foot inside the house and she reveals some kind of psychic talent. I don't know if she says it out of habit or if my silence suffices. She no longer even stops to tell me or gets pissed off. Nor do I try to defend myself. I'll go to sleep, then out drinking in the afternoon. I'd like to find a girl to do it with, but this is a hope I no longer even entertain. I haven't had a girlfriend for years. I've loved a few, from my teens to the last one when I was around twenty. We even talked about marriage, a house together, a family. Then it all became a charade, an imitation of those around me, my father, my brother. It was a very painful farewell. She was the first witness—outside my family—of my rapid trainwreck. It all happened one evening, one of the last in our relationship. Seeing no other escape, I wanted to end it all, but thinking about suicide and carrying it out are two entirely different things. I limited myself to despair, to smashing dishes and trinkets, to punching walls. I hurt myself, something I've always excelled at. It was the first high note, the first sound emitted by my increasingly unmanageable suffering. She watched on as a lover. Perhaps nothing worse happened thanks to her. A few days later I told her that things couldn't continue between us.

I haven't thought of her since, at least until recently, only because the past—compared to this ungenerous present—strikes you as a beautiful land, even when it isn't.

"How did it go?"

My mother sits down beside me in the living room. I wonder what she wants to hear.

"I signed the contract. I start tomorrow morning at six. I have to do nights as well."

My mother's eyes—her whole face—now reflect an almost inhuman peak of suffering. You can't go beyond that; you'd tear your flesh off.

"Do you think you can manage it in your state?"

I don't answer straight away because I don't know what to say. I don't know if I can manage it, or if I really want to.

"I'll try, mum. Then we'll see."

I can't keep my eyes open. It takes immense effort to go to my room. I don't even undress. Another benefit of alcohol is this friendship with sleep. I always had trouble sleeping. It took hours for me to doze off, but that was the time of sobriety. You pay the bill for alcohol when you wake up. It's as if the body, unbeknownst to its owner, has done a series of hundred-meter sprints before reawakening. The headaches are gone, along with the nausea. All that's left is the wretched breathlessness and tremors.

I wake up at dinner time. I should take a shower. I go downstairs and find the table already set. My parents now speak a language without sounds, just gestures. Nothing is left to chance, especially nothing to do with me.

A bottle of white in the middle of the table is a clear sign: my parents don't want me to go out. It would be the second night in a row. They're no doubt doing this because of the task awaiting me tomorrow morning, my first day at work. I respond to their wish in the same language, without a sound. I sit down at the table, filling my glass before touching any food. My father regards this as a lash on the back to be suffered in silence. He's a healthy drinker. My mother also drinks half a glass on suitable occasions. Chattiness bubbles out of me after a few minutes. I talk optimistically about everything, about the work I'm going to start, about "this situation" that'll be over shortly. Soon we'll be laughing about it like an unpleasant memory that's now behind us, defeated and overcome. My parents don't respond with the same loquacity and optimism. Now they know that flowing, jovial chatter is merely the beginning of my evening's end, the cheerfulness that precedes delirium. Nothing less and nothing more than a symptom.

Forgetfulness seizes me there, sitting beside my mother and father. I go from empty words to absolute emptiness in perfect, painless fashion.

6

The sound of the alarm clock is an explosion in the compressed darkness of my mind. I only need half a cry to pull myself up, realizing just as quickly that I haven't had enough sleep to give me any sobriety worth speaking of. It's quarter to five.

Before I register the sound of footsteps on the three stairs, my mother and father appear. She's holding a large mug of coffee. She hands it to me still burning; I can barely hold it. As I drink, they stay mute. He in his pajamas stretched tight over his paunch, she in her combat dressing gown.

"I'll tell you one thing. Mistakes can be made. Life waits for you up to a certain point, but from a certain point on there's no turning back."

It's my father who's spoken. Apart from swear words, insults, and curses, deserved gram by gram, it's been a long time since he's spoken to me. I nod without showing any doubt, but I'm the first to disbelieve it. I turn around to get my clothes and start putting them on, trying to hide the balance problems I now invariably have when sober and drunk.

I leave them in the living room, around the table, facing each other. I imagine the words that'll accompany my exit. I've often wondered what they'd do if they were offered a chance to go back, all the way back to that April 26 1974, the day I was born.

It's still dark. Ariccia's town square is completely deserted. There are just a couple of cars on the bridge heading to Rome.

At the only open café, a double espresso in a large cup shakes off the little grogginess that's left in my body. Then I'm off along the Appian Way, deserted and beautiful, beautiful because it's deserted. I arrive in exactly forty-five minutes; the same route in daytime takes at least an hour and a half. The car parks around the hospital are half-empty. The whole of the Janiculum seems uninhabited. It's March, but the morning chill is still bothersome. Before entering, I have another coffee at the bar just outside the entrance.

All over Rome, the light is rising. Churches and buildings are regaining colors left behind in the dark. A magnificence is emerging before my eyes, minute by minute. Beauty without suffering, that's all I want. Instead, it just takes a few seconds to fill me with a fierce sadness from head to toe.

At five forty-six, I punch my timecard for the first time. There are twenty or so workers, both men and women. No one pays me any attention. Interrupted sleep and various grievances—mostly connected to work issues I barely understand—leave no time for those around me to concern themselves with yours truly.

"Take this. The changing room is behind the ER. Go down the ramp and round behind the block. You'll find them in front of you. The guys on the team are already down there."

It's the foreman, Fabio. This time he's smiling at me, holding out a new uniform: grey trousers and jacket, along with a yellow three-button polo shirt with the cooperative crest.

"It's the smallest size. It should fit you. You'll have to wait for the safety shoes. We've run out."

Carrying my uniform, I head towards the changing room, past the ER, already bustling like it's midday with nurses and doctors, waiting parents, prams everywhere. I descend a long ramp. Further down, I can see a driveway entrance with two large gates. In front of one, several workers are unloading groceries. On the other side, next to the entrance gate, I notice a very small building, a sort of little detached house. The door is open and a bright light shines from within.

I've reached the end of the ramp. Here on the left is the walkway that's supposed to lead me to the changing room, but I'm too drawn to that light. If human instincts could be measured, I'd like to measure curiosity: in me, it acts with an uncontrollable force, a compulsion. I slowly approach the little house's green door. Since Bambino Gesù is a Vatican hospital, I envision a church that's always open, a kind of place devoted to continuous worship of God, or something like that, perhaps some work of art to see.

There's only one fairly large room inside. As soon as I enter, the red velvet upholstery jumps out at me. It covers everything with absolute precision, all except the ceiling.

Then I don't understand.

I see without being able to decipher. I read something, but in a language I don't know.

There's a little girl in the center of the room. She's wearing a First Communion dress. Her hair is shoulder-length, brown. The girl is in a white chest, testing it out for some reason.

This is the first thought I come up with.

The girl is fast asleep.

No.

She's not sleeping.

The girl is in the white chest because she's dead.

A ringing in my ears, flushed temples, a sudden jolt from uncertainty to astonishment to emotion, held tight between my jaws.

I didn't know that children die. Yes, they die, but not like this, like that scandal of beauty and exhausted childhood lying at my feet.

Beside the coffin, two figures—elements that arrived God knows when—come into focus: a man and a woman, their eyes transfixed on the girl. They didn't even notice my entry.

I retreat one step at a time, back to daybreak, to the now rampant dawn.

I find myself in a corner, between two iron cages containing dirty laundry. I stand there looking at the wall, but it's her I keep seeing, her face removed from life, her hair carefully brushed. I feel pain in the middle of my chest and struggle to breathe. I use my yellow polo shirt to wipe my face, my hair soaked in sweat.

My mother was right. When she's not right, it's only because she wants to be wrong. This place isn't for me. Children are dying in here and I can't take it. As though in some kind of mirage, I find myself before a bar counter, so long it seems to have no beginning or end. On top—neatly arranged in a precise row—are thousands upon thousands of glasses of white, enough to intoxicate the world.

"Hey, you lost?"

He's a portly man around forty, his face made even squarer by his black goatee. He's wearing the cooperative uniform. He comes towards me and extends his hand. I shake it without doing anything to hide the tragedy I've just witnessed: "There's a dead girl in there."

I stare him straight in the eyes as I say this. He looks me up and down like he wants to figure me out. An expression of utter disdain clouds his face: "Well, what'd you expect? It's a children's hospital, not a circus."

I stay silent.

I want to tell him there's nothing normal about a child's death. Childhood is a land we can treasure in later years. It's that little bit of joy we humans get to experience, not the place where we end our lives. But the craziest thing of all is that my colleague is right.

This is Bambino Gesù Children's Hospital. Where there's illness, there's also death, and here it doesn't come to toothless octogenarians, to junkies, to people stricken by disease but with a lifetime behind them. No, here it comes to children.

"Come on, the others are waiting for us."

He walks towards the changing room without a backward glance. After a long corridor between the boundary wall and one of the hospital buildings, we reach the changing room.

Inside, there's a series of lockers, a few chairs, the mingled stench of fresh and old sweat. There are two guys on the chairs. The first gets up as soon as we enter, holding out his hand like he's brandishing a weapon.

"Claudio, pleasure."

He doesn't resemble a cleaner. From his hair to his freshly shaven jaw, he looks like he's just stepped out of a beauty salon.

The other guy hasn't moved from the chair he's slumped in. He doesn't look Italian. He has olive skin and elongated eyes behind prescription glasses. He raises a hand in greeting. Just the sight of him inspires slowness. He reminds me of a sloth.

"Luciano."

"And I'm Giovanni."

The last to introduce himself is the one who came looking for me. He has the sourest face of all. He gives me a long stare.

"Let's see if you remember our names."

I think about it, repeating with a fair degree of confidence: "Giovanni, Claudio, and Luciano." I point to each of them as I say this.

Giovanni smiles and pats me on the back: "Great. Since it's your first day at work, you can buy everyone a coffee." He points me towards a locker.

My three colleagues talk and joke among themselves. I don't have much time for them or for taking offence. The vision of the little girl haunts me. Her face, those of her father and mother. I can't help identifying with them, they who conceived, waited, raised, and loved, only for it to end like that, in that unspeakable way.

I'd like to confront those who criticize my attitude, who brand it as self-destructive. Isn't that just what life is? As always, I end up cursing myself for how I am, for how I'd like to be. Why does other people's suffering affect me like this? Why can't I protect myself?

I only wake up when I reach the glass entrance to the ER. I hadn't seen myself with my uniform on, so completely grey I resemble a mouse. I take a good look at myself. Aside from a slight belly, there's nothing especially abnormal about me, at least that's how it seems to me. A normal guy through and through. At first glance, even my lifestyle isn't obvious.

We enter the café next to the ER. Earlier, I saw another one halfway down the main avenue. The café in question is a little ten-by-ten-foot room. People are crammed inside to an almost inhuman extent. Everyone is joking and greeting each other. The three guys on my team know everyone, from doctors to nurses to nuns. For each of them there's a good morning, a quip, a promise of a 'once-over.' I couldn't care less what this means. It's a challenge to reach the counter. I pull out five thousand liras, then the espresso arrives, gulped down piping hot.

We slip into the passageway on the first basement floor, heading—the others tell me—to Fabio for the shift instructions. There are several colleagues outside the office. Another procession of greetings and banter, of promises about this or that job that needs doing. I now have enough facts to deduce that this is some kind of team with superpowers. Superheroes grappling with special cleaning tasks. The mission that Fabio assigns us is to clean the playroom windows. My teammates accept it with a smile. Apparently, it's an absolute walk in the park.

The windows are no less than fifteen-by-fifteen feet with huge panes set at an angle, some Disney character decals on the inside, and traces of color everywhere. In the playroom—like little fish in an aquarium—are many children absorbed in different games, parents, a few people in scrubs.

"Felt-tips are no problem, but the wax ones really piss you off."

It's Luciano, the sloth, who has addressed me.

"Where are you from?" My curiosity about his complexion and features is too strong.

"Sardinia. Bosa Marina."

Although I've never seen this place, it's a name with a family link: "My grandfather was from Bosa, but I never met him."

This very remote common ground makes even Luciano smile: "Bosa is glorious." He says this with chilling nostalgia. "But there's no work there. All my friends have become junkies."

I nod. Who knows what he'd think of the guy standing before him if he knew his circumstances. Luciano wins the title of the first human being to have had a dialogue with me worth speaking of. That must be why Giovanni and Claudio paired us together: I soap the windows with a telescopic rod ending in a sponge strip; he passes the window wiper and dries them with quick, precise movements. Before long, the huge pane is so clean it seems to have vanished. We start on the second window, but we're distracted by the sound of Giovanni's mobile ringing. Fabio arrives soon after. It was him calling. The two of them mutter together, looking at me insistently. I can almost see a sneer on their faces, but I'm not sure.

"They've messed up the toilets over by the ER. You go, Dan."

I follow Fabio, wondering what kind of "mess" awaits me. We enter a very old building I haven't come through before. The long corridor is interrupted on the right by a huge door, the hospital chapel. I quickly glance over. A few people are praying inside. The motionless crucifix has two lit candles on either side. A few bouquets of fresh flowers at its feet scent the air. There are so many questions I'd like to ask Christ. The first concerns the last thing I saw, the child I carry in my eyes: what loving design can this death possibly be attributed to? What lofty path, invisible to us humans, justifies this life taken from the world? There's no possible reason for that innocent's death, not one that I can comprehend.

We reach the entrance to the public toilets. A girl from the cooperative has put the trolley sideways to prevent anyone from entering. She looks tired, but her pretty face seems unfazed.

"I couldn't do it, Fab."

Fabio nods and we both enter. The moment we set one foot inside, we're mauled by a terrible stench of shit and we're still in the sink area.

"There were a couple of tramps here earlier. The ones who sleep on the steps below." The girl offers this useless detail without stepping back inside, then seems to notice my presence.

"You must be the new guy. I'm Paola."

I tell her my name without even turning towards her. Fabio kicks open the bathroom doors, one at a time, until the second last. We both immediately put a hand over our mouths.

My years of debauchery have granted me all kinds of hellish visions, but a sight like this is new to me. An explosion of shit. Shit covers every corner of the bathroom, even the walls, at least three or four feet up from the floor. Fabio immediately retraces his steps and I follow. As soon as we're outside, we start gasping hard to get the unbearable stench out of our lungs and throats. Then he walks over to a garden hose lying on the ground and attaches it to a tap on one of the sinks.

"Here. I'll get Paola to leave you the trolley so you've got everything."

They leave me there holding the hose. The trolley stands before me filled with detergents and disinfectants. I fling the hose down, cursing the day that began badly and continued worse.

I'd like to cut and run. After all, what the fuck do I care about public toilets flooded with shit at Bambino Gesù Children's Hospital? Besides, what crime would I be committing if I ran off? Absolutely none. I stay like that for a few minutes. I light a cigarette but start gagging and immediately toss it away. The stench has arrived out there too. I don't even want to think about inside. Eventually, I'm not sure why, I decide to stay.

I go over to the trolley, taking three pairs of gloves. My fingers are covered with cuts, plus I bite my nails until they bleed. I slip on one glove after another—three on each hand—then cram as much air into my lungs as I can. I finally enter.

When I fully open the tap, a violent jet of water bursts from the hose. I reach the horrific toilet after I've flooded everything with water, even the ceiling. I'm enjoying it. There's something vandalistic, thuggish about the way I'm doing it. From a safe distance, I point the jet at the offending toilet. Meanwhile—to breathe—I press the crook of my elbow over my nose; this way, I hardly smell anything. The force of the water strips off the shit. I'm convulsed by gagging, but I manage not to vomit. I feel strangely fine, perhaps I've found my life's work: scouring tramp shit from public toilets in a hospital. Most of all, nothing pains me anymore. Amidst the strain, sweat, and stench, I can even forget the little girl's face.

Now it's bleach time. I pour out a five-liter jerry can like it's holy water, blessing the whole bathroom. I grab a broom from my steed—the cleaning trolley—and start scrubbing the walls with all my strength. I can't help smiling. Those asshole colleagues are probably laughing at me, imagining God knows what struggle, what drudgery I'm facing thanks to the mission they've assigned me. Never underestimate the strength and self-sacrifice of the deranged: if I want, I'll clean the bathroom so well they can eat off the floor. I'll show them what I'm made of. It may end up being my first and last day here, but the way I clean this bathroom will be talked about for centuries. I come out drenched in sweat. One by one, I slip off my three pairs of gloves, rewarding myself with a nice bleach-flavored MS.

Barely ten seconds go by before the other guys in the team arrive with Fabio. Their smiles in the distance seem to confirm my thoughts.

"Finished, Dan?" Giovanni asks me. I gesture with my head as if to say "come on in," and they immediately enter. I can't hear any comments. Honest to God, if they start finding fault with the work I've done in there I'll pounce on them one by one.

Fabio is the first to come out. "Damn, nice job, Danny." He takes my arm and squeezes it. "Now we know who to call any time we get a toilet flooded with shit." He laughs, then the others come out.

"You've made it good as new, Dan," says Giovanni, looking satisfied and nothing more.

"Since you got the first one, it's our turn," Luciano tells me as he heads to the café.

"Come on, midmorning coffee is on Luciano."

Time has flown by: it's past eleven, astonishing.

At one o'clock, we start doing odd jobs. We move some cupboards to the Salviati pavilion, then tighten some shelves at the Ford. The nun who called us returns the favor with an espresso from the machine, my fifteenth since I opened my eyes still drunk.

At ten to one, Giovanni makes his way to the changing room. The shift is over, time to change. As we walk, he beckons me close.

"I don't know if Fabio or Antonio told you, but we work fixed shifts unless there's overtime stuff. We do Monday mornings and Tuesday and Wednesday nights from eleven to six, so tomorrow you'll work your first night. Forget about rest and recovery on Thursday; we do two to eight in the evening. On Friday, it's five to midnight; there's the regular once-over of the blood collection center. Got it?"

I nod, though I've no idea if this fine speech will concern me or not. We've reached the ramp to the ER. The second act of my suffering is written down below.

A hearse. There are at least a hundred people. We pass by just as the small white coffin leaves the little house, carried by the mother and father. I have to play it cool and smoke the cigarette in my mouth like everything is normal, but I don't know if I can. My eyes sweep over everyone's faces, then linger on those of the mother and father.

Fathomless, immobile ravines.

I punch out at one fourteen. Perhaps my first day of work will be my last, but right now nothing really matters to me. I just have a consuming need to drink. I have to erase my memory as much as possible, to forget the whole day.

It's beautiful weather. I walk out of the office corridor with my hands in my jeans, starting to mentally select the various bars I know in Rome. I choose one in Testaccio. A quiet, secluded spot.

Knock knock.

I hear the sound of rapping knuckles as I walk down the hospital avenue.

Knock knock.

It's coming from the pavilion in front of me. I start looking around for its source.

Knock knock.

One by one, I scan the rows of windows above me.

Knock knock.

I eventually find the owner of the rapping knuckles. He barely reaches the window. He's a child around ten years old with hair as dark as his skin and an aquiline nose. I've no doubt where he's from: definitely South America. It takes me a few seconds to notice the transparent tube attaching him to an IV.

The boy and I look at each other, then he points at me. I see his lips slowly spelling something out. At first, I don't under-stand. Then I do. The boy, one syllable at a time, is calling me a 'CUCK-OLD.' To remove any doubt, he makes the sign of the horns, clenching his right hand into a fist with his index and little finger fully extended. Then he turns serious again, staring at me.

I leave him there at the window and walk on, more bewil-dered than anything else.

7

I wake up as if a starting pistol had sounded. I'm short of breath, suffocating. It takes at least a few minutes to regain a modicum of normality and to work out where I am.

I haven't woken up in my bed, but in the car park where I left the car about five hours ago. Monte Testaccio is right in front of me.

The last thing I remember is getting out of the car. Other fragments slowly surface: the barman's smiling face, the same face poisoned by anger as he kicks me out. And that's all.

It's nine in the evening. I get out to rinse my face at a drinking fountain. A violent cramp immediately assaults my stomach; in the last twenty-four hours, I've only swallowed coffee and wine. I'll eat at home, not least because I don't even have a hundred liras left in my pocket.

The house already seems asleep, but the click of the light switch is enough for my parents to come down to the kitchen. My mother says nothing, goes to the fridge, and takes out a plate covered with another plate: "This is what I left you for lunch."

She places it on the table without another word. I sit down trying to hide my hands and arms, the parts of my body that most clearly testify to the tremors.

"It went really well. They made me stay longer for an urgent job. They're paying me overtime anyway." I don't know how credible this is, but my parents don't seem interested, a clear sign the pretense has failed. They leave me alone with my plate of ham and cheese. I quickly devour everything, then look around for something to drink, anything. A few weeks ago, I got stuck into a tree-shaped bottle of amaro liqueur at least twenty years old, a souvenir from a trip or something. But there's nothing. I actually never doubted it. In this house, it would be easier to find a gold nugget than an alcoholic liquid.

Aches from the day's work are kicking in. My arms and legs are sore as hell.

I go over to my mother. She almost immediately gives in to the blackmail "lorazepam or I'm going out." I dissolve the tablet under my tongue. I've always enjoyed the bitterness of chemistry, plus a drug dissolved in the mouth takes a lot less time to enter the bloodstream.

But I don't sleep right away. The little girl comes back to visit me as soon as I get into bed. In my mind, words become insistent, pliant. It's been months and months since I've written, since I've read, not even to my many friends scattered across Italy. I no longer write to anyone. Sleep sets in on the words "white," "communion," then darkness.

I played soccer until I was eighteen. I was a mediocre fullback. Technically gifted, but slow, and in addition to the opposition players I had to face another enemy, spectators: just one person in the stands was enough to make me even more awkward. I haven't been in such pain since those years. All my muscles are burning, from my calves to my shoulders, not to mention my arms and hands. I'd like to go out for a drive—to drink—but I just can't. I vegetate around the house, swallowing an anti-inflammatory every two hours. I can sense my mother watching me from afar. She doesn't speak, but I can sense her.

Lunchtime. We're sitting across from each other: she with her eyes on the steaming plate; I with a lump in my throat from the empty hours I've spent.

"What time do you start tonight?"

My mother doesn't raise her eyes to ask me. Ever since the night she and I stood on the bridge, she's different. She seems almost ashamed in my presence, perhaps because of how I saw her in those moments: her determination, her desire to end it all. I don't answer her question. I don't want to go back to that place. Yesterday morning was more than enough for me.

"Actually . . ." I have to find the right words to tell her. I don't know how she'll react to my decision. The toilet I cleaned comes to mind. When I tell her about the shit I had to deal with I'm sure she'll happily accept my retirement from the hospital scene.

"Mom, you have no idea how disgusting it was yesterday. They made me clean a toilet."

She raises a hand to interrupt me.

"We're having lunch."

True, no need to continue. But this information cut off midway makes her flinch, or something. She pauses with her fork dangling in the air. "So, were you good?"

My mother is still beautiful when she smiles. It's been a long time since I've seen one appear on her mouth, even if it's not a full smile. I keep eating, but I know she's waiting for me.

"Yeah mum, I was great. They said I clearly took the job seriously. Anyway, I start at eleven tonight."

My mother suddenly gets up and goes to the kitchen counter. When she comes back, she's clasping a small object. She places it in the middle of the table, next to my glass.

"Look what I found when I was tidying the wardrobe."

A dark pink object, blackened on one side. In flashbacks, images from my past spring to life. Little me with a wheelbarrow and spade. Me again down a very deep hole, my hands bleeding from blisters.

It's a head from a figurine, the first discovery in my career as a treasure hunter. Intact, enormous. I relive the astonishment of the moment I found it in my hand, still smeared with soil. I remember crying out to my mother, her amazement embracing mine. She and I dreamt for a whole afternoon, reconstructing the history of that figurine head, its perilous journey through time, from ancient Rome to the present day. We even imagined the prayers addressed to that deity, the faces of those who prostrated themselves before it seeking help.

In the evening, we showed it to my father. He weighed it in his hand, stood against the light to observe it, then took his lighter and held the flame up to our treasure.

"It's plastic, unfortunately," he told me, as the figurine head—on the side struck by the flame—turned from pink to black. That night everyone—including my sister and brother—felt the disappointment: my treasure had been demoted to hard plastic. I couldn't talk about it for days.

But I didn't give up. It was just the first discovery in an endless series. I've always searched and continue to do so.

Still sore as hell, my stomach aching from the anti-inflammatories, I clock in for my first night shift at ten forty-six.

Fabio isn't around, but the other foreman is on duty, a cube of human flesh wider than he is tall. "Antonio, nice to meet you." He shakes my hand, almost crushing it.

He doesn't add anything and neither do I, apart from my name.

Outside the office, I can hear the sound of the clocking-in machine. A woman in her fifties appears and scrutinizes me from head to toe. "You must be the new guy."

I nod mechanically. "Yeah, I'm the new guy. Daniele."

"I'm Marianna," she replies, continuing to scrutinize me, pausing at my feet. "They told you there are no safety shoes?"

I nod again.

"I'll sort it out for you. Are you a union member?"

"No."

"I have to leave now. Tomorrow afternoon I'll have you sign the documents."

I don't know if it's because of her brash demeanor or her tone of voice, but I find her unbearable. She has something military, intransigent about her. "Do I have to sign documents for the safety shoes?"

She looks at me like I'm simple. "Of course not. It's to join the union."

"How much will it cost?"

"Sixty thousand liras a month and you get everything, including legal cover for any disputes."

"What if I just want the shoes?"

Marianna falls silent, shrugging. Malevolence seldom seen in a human being radiates from her eyes. "If you just want the shoes, no problem. You'll have to be extremely patient."

I give her a cheeky grin. "No problem, I've got these for now. Nikes. They fit like a glove."

Marianna leaves, irritated. Antonio looks at me in amazement. "It's obvious you're new. She's a real hag. Tread carefully."

The little house where I saw the girl is deserted. There's no trace of the grief that unfurled here yesterday morning, aside from a few flowers from the many wreaths. I pick one up and start slowly stroking it, then leave it beside the green door. I can cry in many ways, from the most distraught to the most discreet, almost invisible. Like now. Aside from the tears, I manage to control my face, to order it not to wrinkle for anything in the world. I carefully dry my eyes before entering the changing room.

Inside—along with my teammates—are other guys I've never seen before. The first to introduce himself is Carmelo. He has a nice face and a huge AS Roma wolf head emblem with a gold necklace. Then it's Amir's turn. In chorus, almost everyone tells me he's an Egyptian "pizzamaker" by day. It turns out he makes pizza by the slice in Lunghezza, where he lives.

The last to introduce himself is Stefano. He's the quietest, the shyest. We shake hands and I instantly know why. Stefano and I are bound by a trait, a kind of kinship, a shared blood. Mine is called alcohol, his is heroin. Mine can be concealed, hushed. His can't. It explodes in his eyes, in his gaunt face. Carmelo, Amir, and Stefano are on the same fixed shift, working long afternoons, each with a specific duty. They're the guardian angels of the many avenues that make up the hospital.

Stefano is the first to leave. Just a mumbled "see you" and he quickly slips out.

Carmelo no longer looks so nice as he glances towards the door. "That fucking junkie," he says in disgust. Everyone else nods, including Amir. "If he gets hurt one day and needs rescuing, I don't know about you boys, but I'm not touching him. Not on my life. That guy has hepatitis C and HIV. Probably worse."

I try to distract myself from the nastiness directed at Stefano, calmly removing my clothes and getting dressed again. The comments about him continue, but thankfully Carmelo and Amir go home.

They're done for the day. We've only just begun.

That night, we have the pleasure of giving the cardiology day hospital a "once-over." We fetch vacuum cleaners and wet vacs from our tool room, then the scrubber-dryer, which I finally get to see. It's a kind of heavy iron polisher with a very tough abrasive disc at the bottom.

Claudio buys us the first coffee of the evening at the vending machines; the hospital cafés are closed at this hour. From the banter, especially with Giovanni, I deduce that he's having an affair with a colleague, though he has a wife and daughter at home.

The cardiology day hospital must be at least three thousand square feet. Clinic after clinic, a double waiting room, a corridor of doctors' offices with at least another six to seven rooms. I start work by repeating yesterday morning's ritual: three pairs of gloves to protect my hands, one on top of the other.

First, we have to remove everything from the floor: lamps, bins, chairs, examination tables, everything. This task alone takes an hour and a half. The little energy I have runs out almost immediately; only the scattered pain remains. Luciano and I are assigned to "high dusting," while Giovanni and Claudio take care of the floor. I pull out the last cigarette from the half-crushed pack of MS and light it.

"No one told you about smoking?" Giovanni asks me.

"No, why?"

"It's forbidden to smoke here, even outdoors. Of course, we all smoke but be careful. Don't let anyone catch you. A year ago, a colleague got kicked out for a cigarette."

I'm surprised. "Fired for a cigarette?"

Giovanni nods. "The hospital director hates smoking and that poor guy walked into his office with a cigarette in his mouth. By the way, always wish him good morning and good evening. You haven't seen him yet?"

"No."

"Better you don't."

Luciano and I start dusting the cupboards, pounds and pounds of caked dust. Claudio floods the floor with water and wax remover. It's Giovanni's turn with the scrubber-dryer. He starts it up and the abrasive disc immediately begins to whirl on the linoleum. Giovanni holds it effortlessly, but it's clearly very difficult. It doesn't take much for it to slide away on the water.

"Look, Dan," he tells me. "It can easily shoot off. If you're not careful and you don't know how to handle it, it could end up on your legs. It'll break them in seconds." Giovanni goes back to work. I stand watching him. His attitude seems slightly different from yesterday, as do his words. Now, more than anything, he seems to want to teach me.

At two on the dot, Claudio applies the first coat of wax. He looks like a painter at work on a floor or a master of some oriental discipline. His movements are slow and precise. Not one millimeter of surface must be left uncovered. Claudio finishes in forty minutes. Now we just have to wait for the wax to dry.

My colleagues go off to eat in the changing room; I stick around. I have to take an anti-inflammatory. I'll go to one of the many vending machines scattered around the hospital to find some cake or biscuits, something solid to wolf down before the medicine since I didn't think to bring my own food.

I stroll along the avenue outside that connects the various pavilions. There are very few people around, a few white coats. Almost all the windows are dimly lit. Some are illuminated; you can glimpse movement, people. The walk allows me to construct that place in my mind. One by one, I start to learn the names of its various pavilions: Salviati, Ford, Spellman, Sant'Onofrio, Pio XII. I enter Sant'Onofrio. The vending machines are in a dimly lit area. There's almost nothing inside them and I eventually make do with a hot tea.

"Got a cigarette?"

I jump out of fright, simultaneously retreating. I can't see anything in the half-light. I start looking for the owner of this voice. A guy slowly comes into focus, no older than forty. He has a few days' beard and hair shaved at the sides. He's one of the many skinheads I used to come across at clubs. You could recognize them from their shaved heads and bomber jackets, as well as their usually overt fascist leanings. Like me, he's grown up a little, badly.

"Sorry, I'm all out and I don't know where to get any at this hour." I hand him one from the pack, taking the opportunity to light one myself.

"You work here?"

I nod, though given my uniform it doesn't take a genius to figure it out. "You?"

He smiles, taking a long drag from his cigarette.

"I've got my son here."

We fall silent. I have to return to the day hospital soon to get back to work.

"Six months ago, he came home with a sore foot. That boy never stops, what with his football, the swimming pool, his little mates. Anyway, who doesn't get hurt at that age? I broke my fingers a dozen times." He takes another deep drag and the cigarette glow momentarily lights up his face. "But the pain didn't go away. Days went by, weeks. The pediatrician didn't even want to take an X-ray, and now . . ." A sob takes him by surprise. He does his best to hold it together.

"Now he'll be lucky if they leave the leg from the knee up." There's no stopping it now. He's overcome by weeping, mercilessly doubling over. I'm standing beside a guy I've never met before. I know nothing about him except the calamity that's currently crushing him two feet away from me. I'd like to do something, to say something, but I'm incapable of making any gesture, of uttering a single word. A last drag on the cigarette, a faint "thank you," and the full-grown skinhead disappears up a staircase.

I stand there in the half-light with one hand pressed against my forehead, my eyes. Then I walk on. A sense of dizziness, of immense inadequacy makes me feel small in every way: in age, in height. A child grappling with misfortunes previously only discerned in passing, conjured up like nightmares, but always from afar, like a tidal wave, something possible, yet extremely remote.

I go back to the cardiology day hospital. My colleagues have arrived before me.

"What've you seen? A ghost?" Luciano asks in his blend of Italian and Sardinian. Giovanni and Claudio—each with a floor waxer—have already started applying the second layer.

"Sort of," I tell him, stepping as close to him as possible. "I met a child's father. He started crying."

Luciano looks at me. "You need to get used to these things as soon as possible or you'll get hurt."

Now I'm the one looking at him. There's no irony in my reply: "So how do you do it? Have you managed?"

Luciano lights a cigarette. "Yeah, I've managed. You've got to."

Giovanni and Claudio finish the second coat, slumping down on some benches to recover from the exertion. It's our turn. We start with the outermost rooms. Luciano touches the wax: it's completely dry. We can begin to put everything back on the floor.

It's ten to five. The cardiology day hospital looks like it's just been opened. It's perfect, shiny from head to toe.

Drained from fatigue, we walk towards the changing room. An arm rests on my neck. It's Luciano, smiling at me.

"Tired, eh? It would be nice to hit the hay now. Of course, if there was a girl waiting for you in bed . . ."

"You're talking to the wrong person. I don't even remember how to do it anymore." Luciano's eyes grow smaller and smaller, a suddenly horny sloth. "In here, if you play it right, what with the women in the team and all the nurses . . ." He smacks his lips like he can taste God knows what flavor.

"You? Been playing the field?"

Luciano wasn't expecting this question. He considers it before answering, suddenly intimidated: "Me, no, not at all. I wouldn't even know where to take them. I live with an uncle, a retired priest."

"Living it up, then," I say with playful emphasis.

Luciano nods bitterly: "Yeah, really living it up."

I instinctively take him by the arm. "Don't worry. That makes two of us."

On the way home, as if for the first time on the face of the earth, I see the sun rising with all its power and light. Slow, unstoppable.

From the Appian Way, my Castelli appear in all their beauty, a strip of towns between green and sky. There are moments— the few serene ones—when my gaze isn't external to what it sees, as though beauty is taking it in and protecting it.

My parents are already awake. My father in particular can't stay in bed past four in the morning. He sits at the table with a cup of coffee and the inevitable puzzle magazine. I can hear my mother upstairs in the bedrooms, already hard at work.

I sit beside my father. He doesn't take his eyes off the page.

"How's it going?"

"Good. Tired, but good."

Only now does he look up from his crossword. He's blessed with sky blue eyes. "That's all you've got to say?"

I steal a sip of his coffee. I'd like to give him as polished an answer as possible, but instead only the truth comes out. "It's tiring, but it's not so much the work. In two days, I saw a dead child and a father crying over his son right in front of me."

The conversation ends there. After a few minutes, my father gets up and takes the cup to the sink.

"Strange, eh? Some people try to kill themselves and some want to live, and yet ..."

Again, he spoke without looking at me. He shuts himself in the bathroom.

It's time for a nice hot shower. No matter how much I lather them with soap, my hands still stink of bleach. I can even feel it in my throat, my nose.

I've had problems sleeping since I was a child. As a boy, I liked to observe others sleep. I felt like their protector, an angel sent to watch over them. The paradox affecting me is that there's no logical relationship between my body and mind. On the contrary, the more tired I get, the more my nerves come into play, replacing any other source of energy. They're what sustain me. I should've fallen asleep as soon as I laid on the mattress, but I can't. I toss and turn. My body is tired, but not my mind, never. It's riddled with images, thoughts, and the work at the hospital has given it paths, shortcuts to properly recharge. As usual, it's my mother's lorazepam that saves me. She's been taking it for ages. This sleep disorder is her gift to me, along with birth, anxiety, and much more. She inherited it from my grandmother, probably my grandmother from her mother, and so on. A family tree of neuroses, with roots as deep as time.

I wake up at four in the afternoon. I haven't drunk for almost twenty-four hours and the craving makes me jump out of bed. The expectation that precedes drinking—that wants to end with the first glass—always exhilarates me with the same arguments, ambiguous hopes. Each time, it tells me that this drink will be the finest of all, that next to me I'll find a bit of skirt open to every human pleasure, that everything will go smoothly, with no danger of fights, police, or anything else. It was like that with cocaine too, and further back with every other drug. Now I have years of experience behind me. Now I know. Evil lurks in that expectation. Those are its weapons of seduction to ensnare you. Sin. Like a carpet salesman who wants to put one in your living room, who excels at swaying you, at winning you over, only to sell you a worthless piece of woven fabric.

"Don't even think about going out drinking."

My mother is sitting on the sofa by the front door. God knows how long she's been waiting for me.

"You're going back to work later. How do you expect to show up like that? You use machines. You're free to hurt yourself, just like you do all the time, but you work with other people. If you hurt someone, then what? Have you considered that?"

I could leave the house without listening to her as I've done for years, just like that, but a series of flashforwards nails me to the living room. I see Luciano dead because of me. My mother splattered under the bridge. Me with only one death left.

It's an exhausting negotiation, but we eventually come to an agreement. The steak I devour before leaving is washed down with half a glass of white. A little less, actually. In the meantime, my father has returned from work. He casts his eyes on the bottle in the middle of the table. Swearing, he shuts himself in the bathroom.

My mother gave birth to me when she was thirty-three, that's how much more experience she has than me. Before I leave, she makes me swear—on the lives of everyone in my family, one by one—that I won't drink until I get to the hospital.

I go out convinced of my vow, but every bar I pass dents my confidence a little further. I manage to get to Appia Pignatelli, resisting one mile at a time until the Lungotevere. Then I come to a bar with three windows. Beautiful, empty, just how I like them. It's nine thirty-five, still early. There's too much time before eleven.

I leave my car double-parked. I'm greeted by the barman's beautiful smile.

8

Instead of my white wine, I went for some Ceres beer based on reasoning that was flawed from the outset: I hoped the lower strength would save me from forgetfulness. I've believed this theory—slamming my face against it—at least a hundred times. There's an easy explanation for the short circuit: I respond to lower strength with greater quantity, and there you go. I'm not completely lost, but I'm close. I'm trying to control myself, to pull myself together. The only way is to rest. I still have half an hour.

At eleven thirty-five, I wake up crumpled in my car; I've collided at the traffic light between the Lungotevere and Via Arenula. Still sloshed, I try to get out, taking a few steps, just enough to realize I can barely stand. I was supposed to start at Bambino Gesù thirty-five minutes ago. I'll find an excuse, one I've used many times before: it's the cough syrup. "Damn, I overdid it." Hence the impairment.

When I pick up my timecard, I see it's already been punched at ten fifty-six. Luckily, there's no one around. I stagger into the changing room, but it's deserted. I'll buy myself another mobile phone with my first pay check. I used to have a phone, but it was sacrificed during one of my nights out.

I start to walk along the avenues in search of a colleague, someone to ask where the team has got to, but I have to go slowly, controlling every gesture. If I quickly turn my head, I get dizzy and stumble. Everyone I meet seems to notice my state;

social phobia runs wild in that middle ground between sobriety and drunkenness. I keep my eyes fixed on the ground, but other people's gazes devour me.

Knock knock.

I already know where to look.

He's there. His is the only lit window amidst rows of absolute darkness.

We observe each other for a while. Knock-Knock performs the usual little show that amuses him so much.

CUCK-OLD.

Then he starts with his horned hand, waving it this time.

I look around. Not a soul, and I'm tipsy enough.

YOU'RE THE CUCK-OLD. I wave my fist with two extended fingers, just as he did. I immediately look around. No witnesses.

We stare at each other for I don't know how long. I leave him there.

Pavilion after pavilion, I eventually manage to find my three teammates. They're at the Ford, cleaning some walls covered with plastic paint. They see me coming, but no one comments.

"Sorry, guys. I was feeling sick until a few hours ago, so I finished off a bottle of cough syrup to sort me out. Now I'm better, but I feel half-drunk," I say, playing my part, but none of the three give me any satisfaction. They go on working like nothing has happened.

"We clocked you in. Now get a sponge and start cleaning a wall." I do it without saying a word. I take a new sponge and dip it into the buckets full of water and detergent, imitating the others. They're standing on some benches they've taken from the waiting room. I try to climb onto them too, but—as I take my first foot off the ground—I fall backwards. The sound of my ass hitting the ground rattles the walls.

"They better actually give me those safety shoes. These sneakers aren't non-slip." I attempt to find my balance a little, to coordinate as best I can. Then I try again. This time I've managed it: I find myself on the bench with my face to the wall. I extend my arm to start cleaning, but, just as I do, I get dizzy and lose control. I fall, but manage to land on my side, bumping my shoulder. Just a little, thankfully.

Giovanni and Claudio rush over and pick me up, while Luciano stands watching.

"Cheers, what with the shoes and the syrup . . ."

"Does the syrup smell of beer?" Giovanni is standing four inches from my face. "Listen, tonight we've skipped the once-over on the first floor, and we've got to do a bunch of shitty little jobs. Go down to the changing room and get some rest. But I'm warning you, don't talk to me about syrup again. Next time, I'll smack you in front of everyone. We don't joke around here." I nod, but Giovanni stays put. "You can easily fall from a window or get fucked by the high voltage. A load of people here wanted your job. We've made out like nothing happened, but we won't if you have to be a dick too. Tell me you understand." Now all three are giving me dirty looks.

"Yeah, I understand. Sorry."

"Now go and rest."

They get back to work without another glance at me.

The scent of coffee wafts from my nose to my brain. It's Luciano. He hands me the little cup as I struggle to pull myself up from the two chairs I used as a bed. Giovanni and Claudio are also in the changing room. No one makes a sound.

"What time is it?" I ask Luciano.

"Five twenty."

I start to change, like the others, but that silence, the guilt, pains me unbearably.

"Sorry, guys. It was my cousin's birthday last night and I overdid it. I was embarrassed to tell the truth. It'll be the first and last time, I promise."

But no one pays me any attention. Then Giovanni turns to me. He's changed; now he's in jeans and a sweater. He gives me a very severe look: "I'm sorry to tell you, Dan, but some snitch went to the hospital management and told them everything. The rules are clear. Now you'll be suspended from the cooperative. There's also a risk of the hospital suing you. I tried to defend you, but I couldn't."

A tremendous wave of anxiety rises up from my feet. I think how idiotic I'll look to Davide; he put himself out for me and here's the result.

"What for? Nothing happened." Distraught, I sit back on the chair. Giovanni remains standing.

"We're off now, but you've got to stay. The area manager is coming at ten with the suspension letter."

I lift my hands to my face. Not one thing. I can't manage one thing in this fucking life. Giovanni has returned to his locker.

"You guys also smell that stench of shit?"

The explosion of laughter catches me with my hands still covering my face. I open my eyes and see the three crimson-faced assholes doubled over.

"My God, he shat himself." That's all Giovanni can say.

"Oi Luci, open the window, it stinks of shit in here," Claudio echoes. Luciano doesn't rub it in because he can't. He's sitting down, his eyes brimming with tears from laughter. My expression must be moronic. I look at all three of them in turn. A "fuck you" as big as a house erupts from the bottom of my heart. I should lose my shit and pin those assholes against the wall, but instead I start laughing too.

"Bastard."

In response, Giovanni's eyes light up with a devilish glow. "I'll put this in my CV as one of my ten most successful pranks."

We've arrived bang on six. Time to clock out, to see colleagues ready for their shift, still sleepy, silent. I find Fabio in the office. There's a man next to him holding a new uniform.

"Guys, listen up. This is Celso. He's starting today." We nod hello to the newcomer, who smiles with embarrassment. In his eyes, I'm part of the group. He doesn't know I was in his shoes three days ago.

Fabio comes straight over to me.

"Danny, do me a favor and go with Adriana to the villa. Give her a hand for five minutes."

"Of course."

There's a chorus of salutations from my teammates.

"All you boys about to get changed, listen up. I've got to warn you, there's a bit of a stench in the changing room, but don't let it worry you." Luciano and Giovanni start laughing again, then Claudio, and finally me.

"Assholes," I mumble, as everyone else looks at us blankly.

Giovanni gives me one last glance, switching from laughter to seriousness in the blink of an eye.

"We're clear about that other thing, right?" I nod, though I don't know how I'll manage. It's alcohol that's at stake, not a successful prank.

Adriana must be around sixty. She's an imposing lady. Not fat, but heavyset, with manly hands and short auburn hair the same color as my mother's.

"This cooperative is a revolving door. Someone in and someone out every day. Don't get attached to anyone or you'll end up like me." I don't really recognize her dialect, so I don't know what region she's from.

"Where are you from, *signora*?"

Adriana stops and gives me a funny look. "What do you mean *signora*? That makes me feel old. Just call me Adriana."

"Where are you from, Adri?"

"Abruzzo until I was twenty. Turin for the next twenty years because my husband was from there. Then they moved him to Rome. Now he's dead, and I live with my son. He's unemployed."

"So, you're a globetrotter."

She smiles. I feel like I've known her forever. There's something familiar in her gaze, even in her words.

"Tell me, Adri, what's the villa? I still barely know the hospital."

"What is it? A den of vipers, that's what."

To reach the "villa," we have to leave the site and cross the street. Life around the hospital is already an explosion of parents and children, people rushing along, cars looking for parking.

The "villa" is a magnificent little Art Nouveau mansion overlooking Rome. I'm enchanted by everything: the construction, the location. A place like this must be worth billions. The ideal home for any man who values beauty. It almost seems like the whole city is nothing more than a vast garden spread out at its feet.

At this hour, it's still deserted inside. The rooms have been turned into offices, all very nice and spacious.

"I need you to help me move a plant, so I can sweep behind it. I can't manage on my own." The plant in question is a Ficus so majestic it looks fake. I carefully move the huge pot. Adriana quickly cleans, and I put it back in place.

"Thanks, dear."

A woman's heels sound from the villa's entrance. I hear her walk, stop, then gather speed again. A lady in her forties approaches us, short and slender. She immediately crosses her arms. "*Signora* Adriana, I've told you a hundred times that I don't want you to leave the bin on my desk. Don't make me get mean."

Adriana seems to have turned into a little girl, lowering her gaze. "It wasn't me. It was whoever cleaned last night . . . They put the bins up so they can sweep properly under the desks."

But this appears not to satisfy the woman, who gestures with her arm, pointing Adriana to her room. "Come along, Adriana."

We follow her to her office. She stands in front of her desk and points to the bin on top. "Do me a favor and take it off."

"Sorry, why don't—"

But Adriana interrupts my question with her eyes. She walks over to the desk, picks up the bin, and places it on the floor.

"There." That's all she says.

If Adriana wanted, she could easily send that arrogant twig flying with a slap of her manly hand. I know she'd like to. I can read it on her bitten lip.

"You go, dear." And she winks at me.

It's seven, but it feels like noon in the hospital. A human river washes over every corner, entering everywhere. A hubbub consisting of every possible dialect, every color, every feature. On my way out, I pass the playroom, already full of children, but something attracts me and instantly roots me to the spot. It's the crowd of people there. Parents and children. Lots. Loads. The children, aged from five or six to twelve, all have one thing in common, like soldiers in the same army. They're almost all bald, a mask covering their nose and mouth, a thinness with no home but disease. I try to count them, but give up. I pause to observe a mother, a girl who at another time, in another world, I would've stopped, courted with my awkwardness. I have to make all this normal, I have to live with it, but I can't. Everything belongs to me, and I belong to everything. That's what my heart says, annihilated by this waiting multitude.

On my way home, I see two roads ahead of me, and they're not paved. One is the trodden path. Leave Bambino Gesù, drink to the bitter end, and finish the task of slowly sinking that's been underway for years. The other is to work, one day at a time, strain after strain, from heartbreak—seen and suffered—to more heartbreak. Bambino Gesù is a place of torture, a cursed place, a trench opened by a scalpel, invisible to the healthy. It's a place for people like me. A place that trumps any other pain, chosen or imposed. But quitting drinking is like going back into my mother's womb and being reborn. It's reinventing my freedom without letting it pass through the door of addiction, stoned, wired, drunk.

My father is already at work. My mother is outside talking to a neighbor. She starts scrutinizing me the moment she sees me in the distance.

"Come in."

I slip past her. "Look."

I stretch out my arms and raise a foot. Even sober, I struggle to keep my balance, but I manage. "As you can see, I'm lucid. It's not the usual story of when I start to get tipsy. You've got to help me." My mother listens without betraying the slightest expression. She's heard this speech too many times, far too many. "I don't have the strength to quit completely, but I've decided not to drink during the week. Otherwise, I'll get kicked out, and I care about this job."

She remains impassive, continuing to study me. "Help? I've wanted to help you for years, but only you can help yourself. Until you quit completely, you'll never stop. Even you know that." Her face slowly softens. "And why do you care so much about this job?"

I don't answer. I go and sit on the sofa, but keep looking at her. "Because sick children . . ." I can't go on. I just stare into nothingness, that's all.

"If you don't understand that what you feel is a treasure, not a curse, you'll never find any peace. I know it annoys you to talk about how you feel but try to see it as a blessing."

"During the week, I'll only be going out to work. Just managing to do that would be a big step forward, wouldn't it?"

She seems not to hear me. "Why don't you write about those kids? It might do you good. You haven't written anything for a while."

I instinctively sit up. My mother's words have touched a nerve that I intentionally try to ignore.

"No, mum, those kids are too much."

I haul myself up from the couch. It's nine and in four hours I have to get going again for the afternoon start. I'll try to sleep. I ask my mother—in case I don't wake up—to come and wake me by eleven-thirty at the latest. As soon as I lay my body on the bed, I feel I may be able to sleep, even without lorazepam.

9

My mother calls me at eleven forty. As usual, I spring out of bed, exploding with breathlessness, a terrible feeling of not having full control of my hands, my whole body.

I find her with my father around the table. Strange he's home at this hour. The next moment, the doorbell rings. It's my brother. He's four years older than me and is my exact opposite, though having a brother like me would test the patience of a saint, and I've witnessed his anger—screamed—with tears in his eyes. His visit at this hour is as strange as my father's presence in the house. "How's it going?"

Now everything is clear to me. My parents have called him for extra advice. This has happened a number of times. My brother and sister are the chosen ones, the other two regular guests in my adventures over the past few years.

"Good, can't you see?" I flex my arm to show him my biceps. "Take a look at that."

But he doesn't seem amused. "Mum told me you're trying to quit."

"I'm trying to quit during the week."

"What can I do?"

"You? Nothing. You don't have to do anything."

The doorbell rings again. The family picture is definitively complete. My sister sits beside the others. "How's it going?"

Our act feels mechanical.

"Great. I've decided to quit during the week. You don't

have to do anything since I'm the one who has to stop drinking, not you."

All four of them stare at me. It's amazing how blood—and love—can make you forget the past. Not the distant, but the recent; months ago, not even years. I've vowed to quit on many other occasions, usually after serious incidents like the car crash when I was saved by a miracle, or hospitalizations. Every time, it ended the same way, with the four of them telling me—shouting at me—that they'd never trust me again. Yet here they are, still willing to hope for me, for themselves. Today is different. Only I can feel it with such certainty and the enormous fear of failing.

I arrive at Bambino Gesù at twelve forty. Fortunately, the car journey doesn't take long at all. The Appian Way was almost deserted after the flood of commuters, plus my speed was steadier. Every time I approached a bar, I gave the accelerator a firm press.

I walk along the sunny central avenue to the office. The growing urge to drink has turned into nervousness. This whole "quit drinking" thing is gigantic—a monster that terrorizes me—and the more I think about it, the more I feel like doing the opposite, getting respectably drunk. I struggle to keep the tremors at bay. Every attempt to quell them seems to achieve the opposite result. The only possible solution is to plunge my hands into my pockets: in there, undercover, they can shake all they want.

Feeling a tap on my shoulder, I turn around and find the newcomer, Celso. I only remember his name because of its strangeness. We properly introduce ourselves and start walking together. Celso must be in his forties. He sports a moustache and a haircut straight from the late Eighties.

"Do you live here in Rome, Dan?" he asks, just to break the ice.

"No, I come in all the way from Ariccia. I don't know if you know it."

"Yeah, I know it. Those roast pork sandwiches. I come from further than you. Latina."

I instantly freeze. Taking the Pontina highway every day—there and back—must be some kind of divine punishment. "My God, I don't even want to think about doing the Pontina every day. Hasn't the cooperative got some contracts down there too?"

Celso falls silent and stops opposite the Sant'Onofrio pavilion. He no longer seems present. "I used to work as a printer in Latina, then my son got sick. Over the last five years, he spent more time here at Bambino Gesù than at home." He continues to stare at the entrance to Sant'Onofrio with fierce insistence. "The print shop fired me in the end because I was here all the time."

"How's your son now?"

"He had leukemia. He was at Sant'Onofrio, actually. He died three months ago." He nods towards the pavilion entrance. "We always used to sit in the sun on that little wall. The chapel priest helped me get the job. He talked to the cooperative director, and now I work here."

We start walking again without another word. I've begun to sift through my memory—yard by yard—for anything even remotely close to the story I've just heard. Finding yourself working in the place where illness devoured your child. Retracing sites, memories, hopes that are now dead. What sin could a man have committed to suffer this punishment? Celso walks beside me, unaware that he personifies everything I've always blamed on life, to the point of despising it, of wanting to end it as soon as possible. Interrupted joy. Love tested by death and pain. Celso doesn't know what I'd give to be able to embrace him, to whisper in his ear that he shouldn't worry: his son has only made himself invisible to his eyes, but he's here, in expectant sleep, ready to hug his father again, his whole family, not just for an interlude, but forever. The certainty of this always—which appears before me from time to time—is something I wish I could promise both Celso and myself, though not for me; for those few loves I've always tried to defend in my life, but have only made suffer instead.

We get to the office. It's five to one and the room is packed with colleagues, including many I haven't met yet. On my first night, Luciano told me that the worst time of the week is coming back on Thursday after two consecutive nights. Giovanni, Claudio, and Luciano display exactly the same tiredness. They share several signs of it: a few days' stubble, heavy eyes, and low responsiveness to their surroundings. Only Claudio, the handsome member of the group, seems to have spent a little time in front of a mirror. They all greet each other, but without the usual energy. Luciano, already placid by nature, seems to move in slow motion.

"A right piece of luck knowing the bosses. You must be the guy who got the spot on the team." A chill descends on the chatter. A young guy—tall, at least six-three—has addressed me. His uniform comes up short on his ankles. Marianna, the union rep, stands beside him. I look at them. In my stomach, shyness mingles with nerves, with a longing for my glass of white.

"I don't know anyone. I looked for work and they gave me this job. I didn't ask for it." My voice comes out shaky. The big guy looks at Marianna as if seeking advice. She forces the fakest of smiles.

"Oh sure, it was pure chance. Who cares about workers anyway, right? Let's just say it was pure chance and forget it."

"I've no idea if it was chance or not. I know I'm here to work. I know I asked for help, as many of you must've done at least once in your life."

No one makes a sound. My eyes meet Adriana's. Dressed in street clothes, she smiles at me, and I smile back at her. I walk over to the card rack, clock in, and leave.

There's a swarm of men in the changing room. We have to take turns changing. Our team waits until last. The afternoon shift colleagues are all there. Carmelo is muttering to Amir. They're discussing a head nurse, vile as far as he's concerned. Stefano, on the other hand, seems less spaced out than usual today. I ask him how long he's been working there, but he has no desire to talk. He just tells me he's been at Bambino Gesù for a year, too long. Celso is there as well. He's finished his morning shift and is ready to return to Latina.

Antonio, the foreman, appears at the changing room door. He's out of breath, four corn brooms under his arm. He looks straight at our team.

"Get dressed quick. There's something you need to do right now. Just a little thing, but you've got to hurry. I'll wait for you at the ramp."

Instinctively—as requested—I quickly start getting changed.

"Take it easy, Dan. That guy gets worked up about everything. It'll be the usual bullshit."

We head towards the ramp, taking our time. Antonio is there, waiting for us with the brooms in his hands. Behind him, next to the dead girl's little house, people are bustling around.

"A politician's nephew died this morning. He's coming here to see the body at the morgue this afternoon. You just have to clean up a bit, sweep up the dry leaves. It's no big deal," Antonio tells us, handing us the brooms.

We start with the forecourt, then tackle the long uphill ramp leading to the ER. Both on-duty and off-duty colleagues pass by, including Celso, now dressed in street clothes. He approaches me.

"Why the sudden clean-up?"

"A politician's nephew died and they've got to make a good impression."

Celso stands still, mulling over my words. His curiosity has turned into something else.

"They didn't bother to clean up for my son."

He leaves me with these words, without so much as a goodbye.

Many of our female colleagues perform their work in the wards, a bit like auxiliary nurses. Some bring test tubes to the laboratory, while others accompany the young patients on their rounds.

Cinzia is one of them. She welcomes us to the sports medicine department, where she works a regular shift. My instant attraction to her is extinguished by the look she gives Claudio, which he immediately reciprocates. It doesn't take a genius to connect the dots: she's the colleague with whom my teammate is having an extramarital affair.

There's no linoleum flooring in the ward, just the dear old red brick, while the walls are covered with white tiles. Within an hour, everything is glistening and fragrant. All that's left is the head doctor's room. I ask—order—my three teammates to go and rest or get a coffee. I owe them a night's work. Giovanni and the others gladly agree. They'll wait for me on the ward terrace.

I start cleaning with a frenzy that turns into outright violence. I have to somehow vent the urge to drink. It's mounting like an increasingly unbearable malaise, and there's no medicine to soothe it. The head doctor's room is done in less than half an hour. I admire my work. Every corner is sparkling, perfect.

The terrace doesn't have the privilege of overlooking the Janiculum, but it's sheltered, quiet, almost as if it weren't part of the hospital.

I find the three of them sitting on a bench with Cinzia, each with a cigarette between their lips.

"Done, Dan?" Giovanni asks me.

"All done. You can check."

I sit with them. Luciano lights my cigarette with the Zippo he was playing with.

"Don't you have a mobile? When you didn't show up last night, we wanted to call you," Giovanni asks me.

"I had one, but it got stolen. I'll buy a new one as soon as I get paid." My mobile actually met another end, trampled by the bouncers of a bar where I'd been drinking as they dragged me towards the exit.

"We'll stay here for a while and rest, then around four we'll go to show our faces at the office. Let's take it easy today, though. I can barely stand." Giovanni is the group's leader. It's plain to see. The leader by age and experience. Even his build helps him compared to the other two, who are smaller, little more than boys faced with his 14-plus stone.

"Dan, now we're alone here, in private, who do you know who got you straight on the team? Maybe you can help us out too." It's Claudio asking me, but I can't help thinking it was Cinzia's suggestion.

"Who do I know? No one. A friend of mine knows one of the heads of the cooperative, that's all. I don't know anyone."

"So, who's this friend?" Now it's her, Cinzia, who can't resist. The conversation is starting to annoy me. I very slowly exhale.

"O.K., let's start at the beginning. I don't know anyone in this line of work. What you don't know is that I write. I've met a lot of people through writing, including a friend, a poet, who helped me find a job. The end."

"You write?" Luciano looks at me with a curiosity I've never seen before.

"Yeah, I write poetry."

"You're a poet!" Giovanni is genuinely impressed.

"'Poet' is usually something other people call you. I try."

"Can't your poet friend put in a good word for us too?" Claudio asks me half-jokingly. I spring up from the bench. All these questions are getting on my nerves. Their stares—though I'm used to them now—are something I'm struggling to deal with.

"Guys with connections don't get sent to do cleaning. They land a job in a ministry, in some organization, making five million a month."

"Actually, there are people queuing up to become members of our cooperative. People who'd sell their souls to the devil to join."

My three teammates, including Cinzia, have suddenly changed expression. They look offended. It takes me a while to understand my arrogance, the sheer sense of superiority of my words. The condescension with which I spoke about this work—about the cooperative—even touched their lives, as if I'd called them mediocre to say the least.

"I know, I know. It's one of the top cooperatives in Italy. Last year it even got a big award."

My recovery attempt seems to have succeeded. All four of them nod.

"Sure, it was ranked in the top five cooperatives in a study by a newspaper. I forget the name now, but I'll tell you when I remember."

This brief discussion, however, has made one thing clear to me. There are huge differences between me and my colleagues, bridged only by the affection I feel for them and the hard work we've done together. These differences lie in the dreams we cherish, the choices we've made, the places where destiny has ordained our birth. It would be dangerous to ignore these differences, both for me and for them. Before alcohol prevailed, my dream was poetry, and then—to make a living, since you can't live off poetry—to find a job in communication, like a press office, or in some advertising agency as a copywriter. Cinzia's dream—glimpsed between one cigarette and the next—is to open a lingerie shop in Mentana, perhaps with Claudio. Giovanni, on the other hand, wants to try his luck with his own small cleaning company. He'd only need to start with three blocks of apartments. I take no pleasure in the differences I'm starting to notice. If anything, I feel a strange sense of guilt, something I struggle to explain.

We leave the terrace at three-forty. It's still early afternoon and I've already finished my second cigarette pack. We head towards the office at a leisurely pace.

Antonio—the other foreman along with Fabio—is barely five feet tall. When he sees us coming, he rushes out of his chair and takes Giovanni by the arm. The disparity in inches between the two is almost comical. He leads him to the office, carefully shutting the door behind them. Giovanni's profanity is loud and clear. Luciano gets worried. They must've heard it in the medical records office. It's extremely risky to blaspheme at Bambino Gesù. Giovanni keeps shouting, then walks out, red in the face.

"On Thursday afternoon, at the end of the shift. It's complete bullshit. You're forgetting we're meant to be home on Thursdays, resting after two nights straight. It's your job to say no sometimes, understand? If you don't command respect, how are we supposed to?"

Antonio has become even smaller than his five foot something. Giovanni comes up to Claudio. "Two packs of medical vials have spilled in an office. Guess where?"

They search each other's eyes. "Don't tell me! Infectious Diseases!"

Giovanni nods. "Right."

As we walk towards the ward, a word here and a piece of advice there, my three colleagues manage to terrify me, rather than train me.

"So, they've got everything in there, from tuberculosis to meningitis, and those are just the ones they've identified. We need to be fast and thorough. The less time we spend in there, the better. They'll give you overshoes, scrubs, a face mask, and a hair cap."

At five, after putting on all the customary green gear, we enter the ward.

The rooms where children are admitted are sealed off by a glass door. Many of them are motionless in bed, hooked up to IVs and other machines, while others—the ones who look healthier—watch television or play games. We're met by a nurse and arrive at the offending office in single file. Right in front of us—confined to her room—is a little Middle Eastern girl. She sees us coming and immediately looks curious.

We start meticulously cleaning. The pieces of glass from the vials have ended up all over the place. Under the filing cabinets, the desk. In many spots we're forced to use our hands. Mine—as always—are covered with three pairs of gloves. In addition to the pieces of glass, the room is flooded with the liquid medicine contained in the vials. Before getting near it, Giovanni asked the nurse what it was and only started work after being reassured that "it's an anti-inflammatory". Now and then, I turn to look at the girl. She's always there, deeply engrossed in our cleaning. The nurse has never left our side. She watches in silence.

"What's wrong with that girl?" I ask her as soon as I can. The nurse turns towards her and waves. The girl immediately waves back.

"She was a hemophiliac. She got HIV from a transfusion. We get a lot of them from poor countries."

"The blood was infected?"

"Sadly, yes."

I laugh out of nervousness. In my state, I can't control my emotions.

"Those bastards."

That's all I can say. My three teammates also look at the girl. With the mask over their faces, only their eyes are visible, but it's enough to understand what they're feeling.

We finish in less than half an hour. As we're returning the tools to the trolley, a scream erupts. Never in my life have I

heard a scream like that: it's not so much its strength or duration, but the amount of pain it conveys. A scream just a few
years' old. I can't even tell if it's a boy or girl. We stay frozen to
the spot, motionless.

Silence. Then another, even stronger. I'd like to run away or
get down on my knees. The nurse notices our alarm. She takes
Giovanni by the arm to rouse him, then an even more harrow-
ing cry echoes out. The screams are coming from the corridor
we need to pass through to leave the ward.

A doctor and two nurses are in the medical room.

He's on the cot. It's impossible to guess his age. It's impossible to guess anything about what's left of him. Tube after tube.
From a leg, his arms, his chest. Some bags connected to his
stomach by other tubes. When we walk past him, he screams
again. He's looking right at me. He wants something I don't
understand. Maybe he wants me to help him. I can't give him
anything, do anything. Luciano drags me away.

I find myself outside with the others. Piece by piece, we remove our green armor. All four of us are in shock. Giovanni—
disregarding the ban—lights a cigarette right in the middle of
the avenue.

"And they talk to me about Jesus Christ," he spits through
the smoke. Luciano and Claudio nod.

"But when you think about it, there's no other option." I
hang onto my reasoning as I try to get the screams still exploding inside me out of my head. The other three stare at me. "Let's
at least hope there's a heaven for these children."

Giovanni seems displeased with my words. He gets up in
my face. "So, where's this God's justice? Look at this place.
How many scumbags should die before they're born, but live
to ninety instead. A lot of these kids won't even make it to their
first sin."

Giovanni walks on and the others follow behind.

God is no friend of mine. I've often sought him, perhaps

at the wrong times, in the wrong places, but I feel his hand in the beauty of things, in the questions that love makes me cry out. He's also played a part in my very swift decline. I don't know how many of us are out there, but I belong to the category of those who see him in the majesty of things, without feeling warmth in their hearts. A hateful thing. But while life has always seemed pointless to me without a design for us, now, at Bambino Gesù, it simply seems unacceptable. In here, God's hope can't possibly be denied. In here, a godless person can do nothing but hope for the opposite of hope, wishing for the death of all these children, as soon as possible, so they're at least spared a little pain before the curtain falls.

We change in silence. My three companions are pitifully tired. I don't think I've ever seen such broken human beings. By contrast, I'm getting increasingly skittish, twitching at every little thing.

"Know what I'm going to do now? Order a pizza at home, then bunk down. I'll sleep until six tomorrow." Giovanni punches the four cards, one at a time. He already seems to be savoring his pizza. "A nice sausage and mushroom one, then nighty night."

We say good night outside the office and go our separate ways.

When I get into the car, it's twenty past eight. Now comes the hard part. Forget work, forget fatigue. Now I have to placate the beast inside me.

10

I have to focus on something specific. I start counting the trees on the roadside, switching to the white cars I pass, then all the Mercedes. But nothing can wrest me away from the urge to drink. Why should I give it up anyway? Bambino Gesù has done nothing but confirm the insane futility of everything. I'm right. I've always been right. It's better to paint the town red, to go from life to death to the sound of white wine. In fact, the mere existence of that "Baby Jesus" hospital, of the little Christs who spend their lives in it, should be enough for the entire human race to scrupulously annihilate itself. A nice toast right in God's face.

But I can resist.

I get home exhausted. From noises to voices to colors, everything seems amplified by a hundred. I eat beside my parents. They see my state and say nothing. I swallow food. Everything looks dry, coarse. My mother puts a lorazepam pill next to my plate. I didn't even ask her for it. I watch the spectacle of my hands lifting it to my mouth. The tremors come in waves, subside, then resume. My mother and father can't endure it. She's the first to rise.

I wake up breathless, as usual. As soon as I sit up and properly stretch out, I can feel something new, from my leg muscles all the way up my back. My body—with the shock of physical labor—seems reborn, possessed by a forgotten strength. The surprise is short-lived, chased away by the urge to drink. I see a magnificent finish line ahead of me. Today is Friday. Tonight, at midnight, give or take a minute, I'll have finished work. The week will have ended, and then it's party time. I can already taste the night out.

But I have to get there. There are many, many hours to go. I need a distraction, something to take me to my five o'clock shift, and it's only a few minutes past nine.

I end up wandering around the town on foot, strolling for half an hour, the time to have a couple of coffees and to lose myself, as usual, before the viewing area. Ariccia lies in the Alban Hills and faces the Tyrrhenian Sea. On cold days like this, perhaps one of winter's last sorties, the sea seems to loom above it. This is my panorama. In recent years, nothing has given me peace without wanting something in return, except for this.

I get home to find that my mother has placed a bottle of valerian—still in the pharmacy bag—in plain view on the kitchen table. I open it and swallow half the contents. The little pills are sweetish, no relation to the intense bitterness of chemistry, the one I love.

It's midday, still midday. A couple of times I get the impression that my brain is sending a message to give in, to dash to the first open bar, but my body doesn't seem to receive it. I find myself in my room. Nothing draws my attention. I pause before a large chest containing my years of poetry. Everything is inside: the endless correspondence with poets who have now become friends, articles, reviews, piles of manuscripts, notes, verses. There's also the diary with all the addresses, all the telephone numbers. An idea strikes me.

Davide immediately replies. Though I've been involved in the poetry world for a few years now, talking to him, as well as to other poets, still makes me uncomfortable. Social phobia comes easily in any situation, so it effortlessly explodes when I'm around people who are older and more cultured than me. I even struggle to curb my dialect, regarding it as a stain. Davide is full of questions. He tells me to stay strong, then the conversation turns to Bambino Gesù, the children, how agonizing it is to see them crushed by suffering. I also tell him about my first day, the baptism before the dead child.

"You're a poet. You've got a weapon."

I tell him yes, of course, even though in my view the words of poetry and the suffering I've witnessed correspond to two different units of measurement. The suffering is too great, the words too small.

The phone call with Davide has the power to restore my strength a little. I actually have too much strength, but it's an uncontrolled energy that constantly turns into agitation, into anxiety, which no relaxation technique can allay for more than a minute.

I clock in at four, an hour before the start of the shift, but never mind. On Fridays, the team has a regular shift in the transfusion center. I've never been there and I don't know how big it is. All that matters is that time behaves itself and takes me to midnight as soon as possible, then the fun will really get started.

To kill time, I start strolling down the avenues. Now that five days have passed, I'm finally starting to get my bearings. I don't just mean places, but also faces, situations. Everything is slowly becoming familiar. Ultimately, Bambino Gesù isn't so different from Ariccia, my town: a long central street with buildings along it, a church. Instead of townsfolk, there are child patients here, that's the only real difference.

At the entrance to the clinics, I see a young woman coming towards me with the sun behind her. Her figure gradually comes into focus. She has very short blond hair that suits her face: perfection, with those blue eyes, that nose, that mouth.

Up close, she's a madonna. Stunning. Just the right height.

Dressed in black trousers and a white turtleneck, the perfect frame for her body. As she passes by, I see the hospital timecard hanging from her neck. There is a God. The madonna works here. I have to find out where as soon as possible. My colleagues will definitely know.

The clock strikes ten to five when I step into our office. My three teammates are there together with another dozen colleagues. The almost twenty-four hours of rest are clearly visible. They've regained their usual appearance, as well as their good spirits. They see me coming. Luciano stands up.

"Here comes the poet," he tells everyone. They're all immediately curious. I don't know if he said it to take the piss or good-naturedly. The difference eludes me. I scowl at him anyway, but now the stone has been cast. There's a chain explosion of "Really?" "Seriously?" and "Wow!" My colleagues' eyes are curious. They don't know how much I struggle to cope with them all.

"Come on, leave the poet alone. He's embarrassed." It's Giovanni who ends the situation. I give him a quick nod of thanks. Only one of them remains with her eyes glued to my face. It's Adriana. There's an intent in her gaze, a request, but she doesn't seem to have the courage to speak to me. Who knows, maybe she writes too. There are six million poetry writers in Italy. We could stand in the elections and win them.

After changing, armed with all our equipment, we find ourselves in the connecting corridor on our way to the blood collection center. Friday hangs over everyone, albeit in different ways. Giovanni will go to bed after his shift. He has to get up at five tomorrow to go fishing with some friends. Claudio has to stay home with his wife and daughter. He says this like it's a punishment that God has inflicted on him, without noticing Giovanni's gaze, nor Luciano's, nor perhaps even mine. Luciano, finally, would like—to fuck—to do a thousand and

one things, but he'll go home as always. His uncle is very appre-
hensive and doesn't leave him much time to enjoy himself. Both
Giovanni and Claudio reproach him. He shouldn't let himself
be bossed around like a child at his age. Then it's my turn. They
ask me how I'll spend Friday night, the weekend. I answer with
a shrug. I don't really know. I can't tell them I'm waiting for
midnight like it's New Year's Eve.

The blood collection center has a long corridor, three fairly
large doctor's offices, and a huge room full of chairs where
blood samples are taken. Armed with a scraper, a kind of spat-
ula that ends in an interchangeable blade, I start to remove the
dirty wax from the linoleum skirting in the corridor. Every five
yards or so, I get up to stretch my back and rest my legs. It's not
the exertion that bothers me, so much as the pungent smell of
the wax remover. The absence of alcohol seems to have height-
ened my senses a hundredfold. Time flies by. It's now nine and
the first coat of wax is done. Giovanni and the others go off to
eat. I prefer to hang around. Observing is my real job, the one
I didn't choose, but was assigned at birth, and the half-hour
break allows me to feast my eyes. As soon as I step outside, I
notice that the bar right next to the hospital is still open. The
craving instantly raises my heartbeat. I could pop out, have
my drink, and be back here in less than five minutes. I'm de-
terred by the security guard's presence at the entrance gate: he
knows everyone and could get me in trouble. I eventually force
myself to get yet another coffee. In the evening, it's common
to come across parents preparing for the night they have to
spend beside their hospitalized children. Many rooms are fur-
nished with armchairs. In others, the parent has to bring their
own things, hence the baby bouncers. You see some with small
televisions or radios, food supplies of every kind and origin.
From their faces, their bodies, it's easy to discern the nature,
the magnitude of what fate has dealt them through their children. Some no longer look alive. They walk listlessly with no

light in their eyes, living dead who trudge on without even a future awaiting them.

Knock knock.

I freeze. Now my eyes know where to turn. Knock-knock is wearing light grey, almost white pajamas. His dark face looks even darker. Strangely, tonight he doesn't start with his usual lip movements. He seems more excited than usual. With one hand, he signals me to wait, then vanishes.

He reappears holding a sheet of paper, resting it—with difficulty—against the windowpane. At first, I can't make it out. It takes me at least a few seconds. The Earth is drawn on the sheet with its colors of water and sky, brown and green. Around the Earth, Knock-Knock has sketched some little red beings. From this distance, I can't see clearly, at least not at first. The little red beings are actually dozens of tiny horns. As soon as he sees that I've understood the whole drawing, Knock-Knock tosses it aside.

CUCK-OLD. He makes a sweeping motion with his arms, drawing the biggest circle he can, and points at me, YOU, repeating it a couple of times with just his lips. He stands still, staring at me.

I think I've guessed the charade. I communicate the solution to him using—as always—his silent alphabet of gestures: I'M THE BIG-GEST CUCK-OLD—and I imitate his circular gesture—IN THE WORLD?

He nods, still without betraying the slightest emotion.

Then I make three circles with my arms. YOU TIMES THREE! I answer with my lips. We both stand still.

We start laughing at the exact same moment. Knock-Knock has the whitest teeth I've ever seen. They gleam in the middle of his dark face. Even his eyes laugh. What's wrong with Knock-Knock? I've never wondered. From this distance, he looks like a healthy child. As soon as I get the chance, I want to know why he's here.

I wave him goodbye, with horns of course. He immediately looks sullen, turning serious again. He doesn't want me to go. I wave again. In response, he leaves the window.

The countdown has reached the final hour. It's eleven. Giovanni and Claudio are putting the last desk back in place. The once-over of the blood collection center is complete.

"If you want to go, no problem. I'll clock you out." Luciano's tone of voice is subdued, like everything else about him. A guy his age—a guy who works his ass off all week—deserves a bit of fun too.

"Listen, how about we go out together sometime?" Before even finishing my sentence, I start regretting this impulse. What would I do with him? Where would I take him? Without alcohol I no longer have any life whatsoever.

Luciano welcomes my offer with a big smile. "Sure."

I leave the others outside the office after we exchange the customary salutations, wishing each other a good weekend. My first week at Bambino Gesù is over. If I had to calculate its duration as I experienced it, I wouldn't be talking about a week, but at least a month, maybe two. Actually, I feel like I've known this place for years, as well as my colleagues. Everything strikes me as remotely familiar.

As soon as I come out of the underground walkway, I pass a gentleman in his seventies. He has a slightly stooped back and heavy gait. His few white hairs are brushed back, but most striking of all are his eyes, which convey a severity, a sternness reminiscent of a schoolmaster from another era. A nurse approaches at a very brisk pace, only slowing as he passes the old man.

"Good night, Director," he tells him. The elderly man responds with a nod but doesn't dignify the nurse with a glance. This is the director, the feared, hated, cursed director. In just one week, I've heard so much resentment directed towards him that it's a miracle he manages to survive. I'd already been told he stays at the hospital from very early in the morning until late at night.

The hour has finally come. Let the festivities begin. My pace quickens on my way to the car.

In the end, I don't even reach it. I slip into the bar across from the hospital. There's no one around. The barman knows me now, so I ask for a beer: I've just finished my shift, don't I deserve it? The bottle of Ceres is empty when it reaches the car, parked no more than ten yards from the bar.

As I set off, I switch on the stereo, turning up the volume until the bass is distorted. Less than five hundred yards away, I stop at my first station, the bar in the square just below the statue of Anita Garibaldi.

"A glass of white."

I arrive at Viale Marconi feeling euphoric. I dump the car as it pulls up in front of a bar stuck in the Eighties. It's closing, but I still need it. Second. Followed by the third white. On Via Cristoforo Colombo, why not drop into Palombini? Fourth, fifth and sixth white. The bar is overflowing with people, girls of every type and beauty on dizzying heels, wearing dresses in every possible color, invariably short. I blow a few kisses to a brunette who instantly turns her back on me. Disappointment deserves compensation. Here's the seventh. I light a cigarette outside the bar. Two girls walk past me, one extremely skinny, the other chubby. I approach them and ask if they fancy an orgy. They're speechless. Then the thin one gets pissed, telling me to fuck off. The fat one starts laughing as her friend leads her away by the arm.

"Didn't you see he was hammered?" I don't know which of the two said it.

I head back to the car, but there's another bar just across the street. Eighth. Ninth white. Before driving off again, I stop to piss behind a tree. A mouthful of acid rises up from my stomach. I spit it out immediately, but the foul taste lingers in my mouth. I have nothing except wine in my stomach. I'm hungry. Yeah, I need a nice dinner to celebrate. There's a Chinese restaurant less than fifty yards away. As I walk, I feel the euphoria turn into stupor, heaviness. A Chinese woman's smiling face opens the restaurant door for me. Forgetfulness is hovering over my head. I can feel it. Soon it'll swoop down.

11

I see our neighbor Bruno's face an inch from mine. I turn away and there's his wife Marcella. They're pulling me up off the ground. Then they start carrying me. My father materializes before me and almost hoists me up. We walk through the front door like husband and wife on their wedding day. Then darkness returns.

I'm awoken by a loud thud. It's my body. I've just fallen out of bed. I slowly pick myself up. Half my body—from the waist down—is dripping wet, frozen with urine. I find my mother asleep on the three steps, her back against the wall, a tissue in her hand. I go over to her and slowly wake her. I have to help her up. The sound of cracking bones in her back is accompanied by a grimace. I take a cigarette; she wants one too.

"Sooner or later God might turn the other way, don't you think? You've been lucky so far, but what happens when your luck runs out? Numbers are numbers. Once, twice, a thousand times, but eventually you'll pay for everything one night. Maybe you'll hit a tree and only kill yourself. Maybe you'll survive and kill one of the parents you see at Bambino Gesù, the ones you feel so sorry for. Anyway, these conversations are useless. It's been years now."

I don't say a word. I just make a gesture of assent. Her eyes wander to my wet trousers.

"Go and take a shower."

Stationary under the jet of water, I try to wrest something from forgetfulness. I manage to retrieve a few fragments: the vomit under the table in the Chinese restaurant, the disgusted look of a woman sitting nearby, another flashback immediately after—who knows where—of two young guys dragging me, but I can't reconstruct how and why. Then the last. The huge cross-roads where Via Cristoforo Colombo becomes the Pontina. The red light. Me accelerating instead of braking. The amused cries.

As I gradually regain a little control over my body, I start feeling a very sharp pain in my knees. Just below the kneecap, in addition to the grazing, there's a large bruise visible on both. God knows where I fell. On top of the pain, my anxiety also starts to mount. Many doctors' faces have repeated the same— unfortunately true—fact to me: as soon as it's drunk, alcohol has a very strong anxiolytic effect, which then changes to the exact opposite, triggering a series of violent chemical reactions in the brain. Essentially, my head goes from peace to war, along with my heart, every nerve.

By the time I return to my room and get dressed, the pain in my knees has become so severe I can hardly stand. My first concern is work; there's no way I can perform normally in this state. Luckily, it's Saturday morning: almost two full days left before my shift. There's time to recover.

Slumped on the sofa, I look for something on television, but can't settle on anything. It's mid-morning. I've gone from bore-dom to sadness and from sadness to despair. The immobility caused by the pain in my knees has made me an all too easy target. Without that pain, I'd be hitting the town, waiting to re-sume the white wine waltz. My mother brushes past me, leaving a letter on the arm of the sofa.

"The postman just delivered this."

The editor of a literary magazine has written to me, inviting me to send him some texts. They're preparing an anthology of poets born in the Seventies and would like to include me.

My mother just happens to still be nearby.

"Good news?" she asks as soon as I lower the letter.

"Yeah, they've chosen me for an anthology. Great."

She awaits every event, every new development, with the hope that a miracle will occur: a suddenly strait-laced, happy son. A just reward for the life she's sacrificed for him.

"Anyway, give it a rest tonight. Last week went well, didn't it?"

She doesn't even answer.

Lunch between me and her doesn't elicit so much as a dialogue, a word. We just comment on *Signora* Patrizia's mozzarella, some street noise from work on the sewers. She's shaken by a violent cough; I pour her a glass of water.

I find myself looking at her as she drinks and hating both myself and time for the old age we're giving her. I've always defended my mother against everything and everyone. As a child, it was a kind of vocation, a natural duty. Once, when I was no more than six years old, a drunk guy approached her outside a restaurant—my father had gone to get the car—and started harassing her. I remember her terror and how hard she tried not to convey it to us children. Now, twenty years on, I can still reconstruct that drunkard's face detail by detail, down to the color of his eyes, of his hair. Just as I vividly remember the furious strength I was able to muster, a six-year-old boy holding onto the legs of an adult, climbing him piece by piece like a mountain, screaming at him to go away, that nothing and no one would ever be able to touch my mother as long as I was around.

I say nothing to my mother of the memories that have overwhelmed me to the point of barely suppressed tears, of all the undying love I feel. What matters is that her cough has gone.

My father always returned smiling from work, even when tiredness encumbered his stride and numbed his hands. In particular, Saturday evenings, like today, used to be a time for celebrating, not so much the work-free weekend—in fact, he never goes more than a day without working—but rather the time he could spend with us, his family.

For my father, as well as for my mother, we children were the only assets to defend and grow. Tonight, my father has come home thanking—for the umpteenth time—his neighbors Bruno and Marcella for last night's "favor." His forced smile collapses as soon as he closes the door. For someone like him, who regards discretion and good manners as his first commandment, I can imagine the strain of that situation. He walks right past me without even a hello.

Evening is approaching. Despite my aching knees, I want to go out. I arrive dressed at the table set for dinner, ready to leave.

"Go and undress. You're not going out tonight." My father's voice booms from his room. He tells me this almost every night, along with my mother, but they eventually have to give in. Aside from tying me up or nailing up the windows, they've tried everything.

"Go and undress, I said." He's joined me. He's close to me now.

"Dad, you know that as much as . . ."

He doesn't even let me finish my sentence. He only needs one hand, just one, to pin me to the wall.

"I'm fifty-seven years old. I've been working since I was ten. I don't want a son like you anymore. Enough is enough." His grip suddenly turns featherlike and his blue eyes lose their focus. My father falls to his knees. I immediately bend over him. My mother comes running and crouches down beside him, but first she stares at me.

"You're a curse. Every night I try to understand what sin I've committed to deserve a son like you."

Over the last few years, I've wrung such harsh words out of my parents that they've even ended up crying before I have.

As soon as he gathers the strength, my father retreats to his room without even eating dinner.

"I'm going to buy a bottle and drink here. It's fucking Saturday." My mother slaps me.

"That's right. Now your hand will be covered with broken capillaries. You know that's what happens to you."

I go out to get wine, but first I stop at one of the town bars. The white slips down easily. After no more than two minutes, I already feel better. Even my knee pain seems to have abated.

From the time I left the house to the time I returned, ten minutes—at most—have elapsed, but there's no sign of my parents. Everything is dark. The kitchen table is still set. I find them both in bed. My father seems to be sleeping. My mother is illuminated by the glow of a cigarette.

"I won't have dinner either. Good night." She turns away.

Remorse runs through my veins from head to toe, but it's short-lived. Without the two of them on guard, I can drink the whole bottle.

Despite how Saturday night ended, my mother has invited my brother, sister, and their families for Sunday lunch. My brother has a one-year-old and my sister a two-year-old. My nephews are an endless source of joy. They don't make me think of anything other than their perfect smallness. I'm especially moved by their little hands. I don't know why, but those tiny thumbs entrance me every time. The atmosphere is miserable. My siblings have learned of my father's collapse. The first look they both give me is pure fire. They'd like to kick my ass if they could.

Luckily, the babies are here. The conversation turns to the baptism of my brother's son Alessio and the church where it was celebrated, now closed until further notice due to a cockroach infestation. Everyone around the table discusses it, except me, simply because I don't remember anything about the church or the baptism. It's not the only ceremony I've erased. The baptism of my sister's son Dario has also been consigned to oblivion, along with a handful of weddings and cousins.

By around the end of the second course, the traditional mood has been re-established around the table, the one that's become part of our family history. A spirit of fun, a desire to play and spend time together. I also take part, or rather I try to. Often my words fall flat: it's as though my voice never reaches my family's ears, though sometimes, thanks to perfectly timed jokes, I at least get them to crack a smile. Everyone except my father. Thankfully, my nephews are there. They readily smile and laugh. Just pulling a face is enough to trigger their delighted singsong. For a moment, their faces overlap with the many suffering children I encountered in my first week at Bambino Gesù.

Understanding what design dictates the choice: one child in place of another; happy normality on the one hand, abnormal despair wrought by disease on the other. My problems all stem from here, from wanting to understand what has been and will always be inaccessible to mankind. Others accept this impossibility because there's no other option, but not me. I can't swallow the statistic that for every hundred children, one has cancer and another leukemia. All a huge coincidence, from the birth of the Earth billions of years ago to its death in the distant future.

Ever since my problem, my family—even on Sundays—avoid putting any drink containing alcohol on the table, and this lunch is no exception. I assuage the urge to drink with food. I have second helpings of each course, digging into dessert in particular. My siblings leave at three o'clock. I say goodbye and withdraw to my room. Sleep quickly arrives. The heavy kind, with a bloated stomach and painful digestion. I'll wake up with a dry mouth and a throbbing headache, but I don't think about the consequences.

I get up at six. As expected, I have all the symptoms, from stomach acid to a heavy head. I'd like to gulp down a nice white. Not necessarily to excess; just enough to welcome tranquility and then forgetfulness. But tomorrow morning my alarm is set for quarter to five for the Monday shift.

My parents have a mug of milk for dinner. I put a pan of water on the stove for a chamomile tea. It's not so bad with lemon and sugar. I'm really making it to send a message to my mother and father. It's our secret code, a deed instead of words.

My mother has received the message. She goes to her room and comes back with the sleeping pill. I'm not allowed to know where she hides them. The sweetness of chamomile blends with the bitterness of lorazepam and the sum of the two flavors produces another. Pleasant, all things considered.

12

It's a windy Monday and rain carried by gusts is falling obliquely. Rome—stretched out at the foot of the Janiculum—reflects the grey sky, gloomy weather that doesn't improve as the light rises.

At Bambino Gesù, every sheltered corner is occupied by parents and children. Some are soaking wet; one woman dries herself with a newspaper, others with tissues. This is humanity, naked and defenseless. In days gone by, I used to carry around a little notebook where I'd jot everything down. Single words, often whole verses. I haven't done that for years.

My teammates are already there, waiting for me with the others outside the office.

"Come on, poet, let's get going." Giovanni greets me with a neat collar. Claudio and Luciano still seem curled up in bed.

This morning, the little house for dead children has a new guest. A dozen or so people are standing outside, all very young. Tears mingle with rain on their faces. They're drenched from head to toe, but they don't care. They speak a southern dialect, perhaps Calabrian. I pass by, keeping as far away as possible. My eyes would like to enter the house; they try, but I forbid them.

In the changing room, I run into Aldo, the tall guy who called me "connected." We greet each other with a nod and undress without exchanging a word, at least until I get a good look at him. Up close, he looks big as hell.

"Sorry, but I've got to ask. How tall are you?"

He instantly puffs up. I must've touched his pride, his best asset. "Six-four and nineteen stone." He grins like a happy child.

"Couldn't you have given a couple of those inches to me? You still would've been tall, and I wouldn't have been short."

He turns serious. He doesn't seem to have understood my joke. I look away embarrassed, my eyes glued to the locker.

"Listen, about the 'connected' thing, don't worry about it, it's not your fault. I would've done the same in your place. Also, Giovanni told me you're no slacker, so don't worry. Everyone calls me Big Aldo by the way, because of my height."

We make eye contact. I wish I could tell this big guy that his words are the nicest thing I've heard in a long time, not only because of the truce they're seeking, but also because they've allowed Giovanni's judgement to shine through. I'm a serious worker who doesn't shrink from hard work, the same as the rest of them.

When I return to the office, I instinctively want to embrace Giovanni like a brother.

"The poet is ready. We can get to work now." We head off, trading a few words with our colleagues. The mood is cheerful; there's constant banter. A hand reaches into my hair, ruffling it. It's Adriana. I keep sensing a request in her eyes, something she can't articulate.

The first spin of the coffee carousel has begun. The little café is jam-packed with people. Cigarette breath mingles with coffee breath, perfumes and deodorants, hairsprays. Marianna, the union rep, is standing in the middle of the huddle, muttering to a nurse with a head nurse's badge on proud display. She greets Giovanni with a nod. I just receive a condescending glance.

It's stopped raining. Children and parents appear on the avenues like a multitude of snails, following an obligatory route past puddles strewn all over the place. Many—as if on a treasure hunt—are holding a map they need to follow, the medical referral with directions for finding the pavilion.

Our goal is to fix the false ceiling in the administrative offices, located in a small, very old building. On the first floor, we find some panels on the ground. The workers have been moved away as a precaution. With the aid of two ladders, Giovanni and Claudio carefully tighten the bolts on the structure that secures the panels to the ceiling. Luciano and I clean them. Within a couple of hours, everything is good as new. A single panel, in a corner of the ceiling, isn't as neat as the others. Giovanni gets right underneath it with the ladder and tries to put the panel back in place, but something seems to be obstructing it. He climbs another rung of the ladder and tries to dislodge it with all his strength. The next instant, a shower of black stuff cascades over his face. It's rat shit, very big rats judging by the size of the droppings. Giovanni climbs down the ladder without making a sound, his eyes closed and his lips pursed tight. Back on solid ground, he starts shaking off the myriad of droppings scattered all over him. In his hair, in his uniform top, even in his ears. He strips completely naked, finding the last dropping in his underwear. He slowly makes his way to the office toilets, soaping his body one part at a time. I and the others give him a hand, especially with his back, which he can't reach by himself. To dry himself, he removes the toilet roll from the holder.

"I'm going to see Fabio now and honest to God I'm going to pin him to a wall. I'm going to lay hands on him, or my name's not Giovanni!" Seeing him so pissed off—his face flushed with rage—is quite a sight. He's started furiously shaking off his clothes.

"They're turning us from cleaners into slaves. These are jobs for specialist companies. Now they're making us do everything." Claudio and Luciano nod in agreement.

"Sorry, I'm new, so there's still a lot I don't know and

understand, but what does that union woman do? You can get seriously ill from something like that. Rats give you Weil's disease."

"She's got her own fucking agenda, Dan. You know the score. If you don't defend yourself in life, nobody else will." Giovanni has answered for everyone. Neither I nor the others have anything more to add.

I vacuum up the rat droppings in the office. They've fallen all over the place. In the meantime, the others mop up the water that Giovanni splashed about to wash himself.

We march to our office and all four of us go in. Fabio's smile fades as soon as he sees our faces. Giovanni places a knotted latex glove on the desk and opens it: inside—like a load of chocolate sprinkles—is the rat shit.

"An hour ago, I had a bucketload on me. We're going to get hurt here sooner or later. If you and the other guy don't learn to say no, then I'll start saying it."

Fabio is speechless. He picks up the glove between two fingers and tosses it in the bin. "You know it's not our fault. It's the cooperative. The contract expires soon. They don't say no to anything."

Giovanni wants to answer but restrains himself. His rage brings out a crooked smile. He storms out of the office.

"Come on, let's get coffee."

At ten, there's no longer a single trace of rain, of the leaden sky. Now it's tepid springtime. In the sun, parents and children wait their turn outside the many clinics. Their bulky jackets—still damp—are drying on prams. Light sweaters have appeared in their place. The bravest even wear short sleeves.

Giovanni's rage hasn't subsided; it's turned into a tense silence, a bad mood. He's gripping the washer-dryer, a large machine he's using to clean the linoleum that connects the Sant'Onofrio and Salviati pavilions. Luciano and I are tackling the chewing gum, a bitch to remove. Claudio is washing some low windows with the wiper. All four of us are in pretty much the same frame of mind.

"Hey!" I turn to Luciano. He immediately points out a girl's ass. Big, more than big, huge, wrapped in a pair of black jeans that are tight to the point of bursting.

"Look at the size of that."

"Damn, too big really."

"What do you mean too big? There's no such thing as too big. I like women soft, really soft. What do you do with skinny ones? Actually, even that one is too slim for me." Luciano must be nearly six feet tall and weigh a maximum of eleven stone. A long, thin beanstalk.

"How do you like them?"

"Me? Normal, small. Because I can't handle a six-foot woman."

As we're talking, I notice a little shoe no more than three yards away from me. I catch sight of a young woman walking away, pushing a pram. I pick up the shoe and rush to bring it to her. The boy in the pram has Down syndrome. I show the girl the shoe. She smiles at me: yes, it's theirs.

The boy has stopped to look at me. I lean over him and grab his leg to put his shoe back on, but there's something not right. Inside his trousers, I can feel his calf, but the foot underneath is missing. I search for it again in vain. His mother bends over me, takes the shoe from my hands, and places it on the pram footrest as if it were part of a set design. Not only is her son missing a foot, but he also lacks a right hand. She's managed to conceal this absence too: from a fleeting glance, you'd think his hand was hidden inside the sleeve of his little sweater.

You only have to observe carefully to be drawn into other people's lives. This corridor offers the full spectrum of the pain that takes root in children. The luckiest ones—blessed with an iron constitution—will spend a morning here, then head off to their own life of fun and games. The less fortunate will contend with a very different suffering and future. Some of them reveal this in their complexion alone, while others bear more visible scars, hideous in some cases. I feel like I'm on a merry-go-round, motion sick. I go from amusement at a girl's huge ass to the deepest sorrow, mortifying pain, an unknown debasement that instantly robs me of all my strength.

The other three have started putting their tools away. We've finished our work. From afar, Claudio raises an invisible cup of coffee to his mouth, then points to me. I know. It's my turn at the till.

At midday, we start replacing the tools in our cabin. Giovanni has stayed behind to talk to Fabio. Meanwhile, we stow everything neatly away. We also have to note down on a sheet of paper any detergents and materials that are missing for the next once-overs. It's the end of the day and I feel an enormous longing for my white wine. The week has just started and it's still so long. I have to wait five whole days to get to a bar counter.

Giovanni joins us.

"How do you expect a shit day to end? With even more shit, right? Lucia is sick. We've got to clean up and dust the plastic surgery long-stay ward." All three of us nod, snorting, then Giovanni turns to me.

"You better not come, Dan. The plastic surgery long-stay ward is grim. It upsets people who have been here for years. It's best you don't."

"No, I'll come. Work is work."

I recall Aldo's—or rather Big Aldo's—words in the changing room. I don't want to let Giovanni or anyone else down. I'm no different from my colleagues; if they can handle it, I have to as well. My sweat increases almost immediately, along with my anxiety. I live in a state of perpetual alertness and this situation is perfect for exacerbating my problems. An unfamiliar situation awaits me and I envisage it as the worst of all possible worlds.

The plastic surgery pavilion is located in Sant'Onofrio, the hospital's oldest wing. If you love Twenties architecture, it's also the most beautiful. On the ground floor, an Art Nouveau stained glass window overlooks an internal garden with a fountain. The floors are connected by a large marble staircase. Our destination is on the top floor, sealed off by a very heavy red door.

The first two rooms are taken up by children with cleft lips. I can't see the occupant of the third one at all. He has something, some kind of burn covering his head and part of his face, but my survival instinct makes me lower my eyes. I try to raise my head, to bring my gaze back up to eye level, but the fourth room makes me stoop again, then the fifth, and sixth.

"Hey, bro." A child's voice stops me, coming from one of the rooms I only pretended to enter. "Do me a favor, bro."

I turn towards the fifth room, from where the child is calling me.

"Are you talking to me?"

"Yeah. I dropped the TV remote under my bed. I called the nurse, but it's medication time." The voice speaking to me seems to struggle to escape from the mouth that uttered it.

I enter one step at a time. The child is on top of his bedclothes. His feet are sockless. From the size of them, I guess he must be about eight or nine years old. His arm and whole shoulder are bandaged. I can't look any higher up. I try to locate the remote control; the sooner I find it, the sooner I can get out of here. There it is. It went flying under the window. I quickly go and pick it up, then place it on the bed, next to the unbandaged arm. I did all this without ever looking the child in the face.

"Thanks, bro."

I'm half a man, but not to the point of failing to look a grateful child in the eye. I raise my head with immense effort. I don't know what accident, what calamity has devoured part of this child's face. Older scars are visible alongside more recent marks, the slow process of giving him back a human face.

"You're welcome." I head straight out.

Only a few times in my life have I encountered a situation that was even worse than how I'd imagined it. This place is a kind of freak show, a circus dedicated to creatures born misshapen or chewed up by events. Here, illness doesn't occur within the shelter of the body, but is outside, exploding or crawling on faces, bodies that are still tiny, deformed, mutilated, in a way I wouldn't wish on the vilest of beasts. If beauty is a gift for the world, who needs their horror? What do these little kids represent? Sin? Whose? Certainly not theirs, these children born with a terrible, underserved misfortune that has to be smoothed out bit by bit, one operation after another. I duck into a toilet, lock the door, and burst into tears. My knees—still sore—buckle. I shut my eyes, trying to pull myself together, but staying there makes me feel better. My tears gradually restore my ability to breathe. Someone knocks.

"You O.K., Dan?" It's Luciano's voice. I move towards the door.

"Yeah. That last coffee was one too many."

Time to rinse my face, to try a few smiles in front of the mirror, just to see if I've regained a little normality.

Giovanni and the others are waiting for me outside.

"Sorry, I really got the shits." I don't know if they believe me. I don't even care. I'm too busy staring at my toes. I only look up again after stepping through the red entrance door.

As we walk back to the office, I think about the strangeness of fate, or rather its razor-sharp irony: not content with merely finding me a job at Bambino Gesù, it also had to get me on the team, in the globetrotters of cleaning, the jacks of all trades ready for anything. Me of all people.

In the changing room, the guys going off duty—like us—mingle with the arriving afternoon workers. The result is a horde of men squeezed into a dozen square feet. The discussion involves everyone. Carmelo is at the center of the gaggle.

"You're joking. Lazio are crazy strong. That lot are going to win the league." Reactions vary according to football allegiance. The majority support Roma.

"Carm, you hate Lazio more than you love Roma. You're scared shitless," Claudio replies.

"You say that, but they'll do it this year. Take it from me." Almost everyone in the room, especially the Roma fans, start making various superstitious gestures. Some scratch their balls, some touch iron, some both. Amir, the Egyptian pizzamaker, also supports Roma.

"Lazio won't win. Chill man," he tells Carmelo, but there's no calming him. The only one not involved in the discussion is Stefano, who is standing before his locker. He looks like he's just woken up. He's certainly spent the night in company with heroin. He occasionally seems to lose his balance. It's like he's changing in the hold of a ship in rough seas.

"Who do you support, Stef?"

He doesn't turn around immediately. When he does, it's in slow motion. "Lazio, but these guys already hate me, so I better shut up."

"Well, if Carmelo finds out he'll get German measles."

"Measles? He'll get full-blown shingles. Wait until you see how red he gets." He points to Carmelo, crimson-faced at the idea of Rome full of jubilant white and blue flags.

We all go up and punch our timecards together. I walk beside Stefano. He tells me about his plan. He and his girlfriend have been putting money aside for a couple of years.

"There's no better job, trust me. You're outdoors, surrounded by flowers and plants. There aren't many good gardeners around. I was taught by a real master. Then maybe you get a job in a place like this and wind up working at the Vatican."

From his words and the dreams he cherishes, Stefano seems

to shrug off the present that wants him to be a heroin addict. It's normal. This is how diseases behave after all. We cling to the time when we were able to imagine a future and wishes to fulfil. Stefano is nice, intelligent, an unjustifiable waste of life. Observing him, I can clearly see what I'm doing to myself, but this doesn't change the facts.

At twenty past one, a succession of at least twenty time-card-punches interrupts all the discussions between the on-duty and off-duty guys. Then it's just a quick "bye." The moment I'm about to leave, Marianna, the union rep, shows up. Her eyes flick to my sneakers, the ones I also work in. After a week, they're practically worn through. She smiles right in my face. She seems so happy. I step past her without even saying hello.

Knock knock.

He's dressed in an acetate tracksuit today. As soon as I look up, he smiles at me. I follow suit, then he immediately turns serious again, gesturing. He asks me—orders me—to stay put and disappears. He comes back with a new drawing and holds it against the windowpane, but someone inside catches his attention. He immediately stops what he was doing with me.

CUCK-OLD. Knock-Knock is just in time to tell me.

I'm in no hurry. Actually, I'm terrified of leaving the hospital.

Knock-Knock is in the nephrology ward. Aside from the fact that it deals with kidneys, I know next to nothing about it. One step at a time, I reach the door to his room. As I enter, my eyes dart to the drawing he was trying to show me before he was called away, a huge black and red rocket complete with the inevitable horns.

"Excuse me, who are you?"

A nurse in her fifties approaches.

"Sorry, I work for the cooperative and—"

"Are you related to the child? Do you have any reason to be here?"

"No. I work here."

"If you've no reason, you need to leave immediately." The nurse's face is resolute to the point of looking brutal.

"I just want to know the name of the boy in this room. I work for the cooperative that does the cleaning here. I'd like to meet him, to know what's wrong with him, that's all."

In response to my request, she makes a noise like an animal, something between a horse and an elephant.

"You think we give out information on our patients just like that? Just because you clean here, do you feel entitled to know everything? Answer me." My embarrassment grows, along with my anger. I feel my face swell with shame, turning red.

"There we go, no answer. Now please leave."

I find myself on the avenue. I'd feel less pain if she'd slapped me. I try to see if Knock-Knock has returned to his room, but the window is deserted.

KNOCK-KNOCK

13

I t's the talk of the town this Tuesday. Sunday's tidal wave still hasn't subsided, far from it. For the first time in years, the city of Rome—the white and blue side—was on the verge of winning the league.

It's the seventeenth of May. On Sunday, Lazio drew in Florence and were overtaken by Milan in the penultimate match of the championship, practically a yard from the finish line. Many Romans celebrated the result as if it were a divine miracle. Carmelo bought everyone coffee yesterday. Some nurses asked him what he was so overjoyed about, perhaps a windfall or the birth of a child.

"Even better. Lazio has blown the championship."

I've been working at Bambino Gesù for over two months now and they've flown by, just like spring, which has prematurely exploded into summer.

Day by day, I've grown increasingly attached to my work and inexplicably attracted to this place, which can kill me with every step, yet make me laugh with a light-heartedness I've never felt before. The balance of my days holds the children's suffering on one plate and, on the other—in an always precarious equilibrium—the relationship that's now been established with all my colleagues. Apart from Marianna, the union rep. In little more than two months, I've worn through three pairs of shoes. She makes no attempt to get me those safety shoes and, for my part, I'm not even contemplating talking to her about signing up to the union.

Something akin to friendship has developed with the others, an unfamiliar solidarity. What they're teaching me is levity, the ability to smile in the face of all of life's pitfalls. And they—my colleagues—have scrapes and shenanigans, struggles here at the hospital and elsewhere that I can't even begin to imagine.

Some have jumped ship to other cooperative contracts, like Big Aldo, who was transferred to a hospital much closer to Torre Maura, where he lives with his mother and father. Paola, my colleague from the public toilets, has also moved on and now works at Ciampino Airport, still with the cooperative. As some leave, others arrive. Aldo was replaced by Massimo, from Viale Marconi; his partner, Michela, is another colleague in the cooperative. I took an immediate liking to Massimo, who does the morning shift. He has a bald head, an unfailingly neat moustache, and a certain aversion to work in general. The thing he's best at is fucking around. When you're with him, everything ends blissfully in fun and games. If cheerfulness were the only commodity on Earth, he'd be enviably rich. Luciano is one of our favorite targets. We take the piss out of him for his insatiable—though entirely theoretical—sexual appetite. After my initial impulse, Luciano has been constantly suggesting that we go out together. I've managed to play for time whenever he asks, but that's no longer an option. Maybe we'll meet up this Friday, though I still have no idea what I'll do with him.

Besides human relationships, there's one thing about my work that never ceases to seduce me every day. It's great to see things being reborn, to make them as shiny as new. It takes effort and determination, but the result is an insult to time, which wishes to have the upper hand over everything, to always be in charge. The most important aspect, however, is something else, and it makes all the difference in the world: my work calms me down. Mechanical gestures—such as those required to wash the floor or clean a glass pane—allow me to reflect without falling prey to anxiety, perhaps because my mind is busy dealing with my body, engrossed in the actions it needs to perform, and can't focus entirely on my current reasoning or obsession. A couple of weeks ago, I even started using the scrubber-dryer. I've never ridden a horse, but the feeling can't be all that different. It's like dealing with a beast. You have to indulge it but—at the right time—rein it in, otherwise it ends up harming you. I have a great relationship with my three teammates. I know them well now, each man's virtues and flaws, both real and avowed. Giovanni is an obstinate ogre capable of bursts of generosity that would put fairy-tale princes to shame. Claudio is—in a sense—the smartest, as much enamored of Cinzia as he's disenamored of hard work. Luciano needs to get laid at some point because he's becoming a pathological case, something for clinics and medicines.

The glass of white is still there. The decision to save it for the weekends is tough to handle, but I'm coping, especially since from Friday evening I make up for it with interest. At home, we travel in two directions. Starting on Monday, my relationship with my parents improves day by day, only to nosedive again on Friday night, or Saturday morning as the case may be. In the past two months, trouble caused in the grip of forgetfulness has been about average. A couple of collisions, scratches and bruises sustained God knows how and where. Tremors ready to return in their precise disarray.

But there's been a change in my relationship with alcohol these past two months, that's for sure. Since I was a child, I've lived with the certainty of the saying "in vino veritas," as if alcohol were a mirror through which we can see ourselves for who we really are, deep down, a revelation of our most original nature. A pure lie. Thousands of years old, but still a lie. The few fragments of these months—those saved from forgetfulness—recall me in a way I've never been in my life. Wicked. A ferocity no longer content to destroy itself.

I have a memory—the only full one—that visits me on nights

of sobriety, when getting to sleep is a kind of mercy that has to be pursued in the dark, even though my body is defeated by work. Piazzale Ostiense. It must've been three in the morning. I somehow manage to resist forgetfulness. There's a wicked, glistening euphoria in its place. Right on the bend of the round-about, I overshoot and hit another car, cutting across it. Three guys—barely twenty—get out, see me alone, and think they can intimidate me, acting like yobs. Little do they know that there's a bundle of pure madness before them, incapable of feeling any form of human pain.

A police Alfa arrives to break up the altercation. As soon as I see them—with the confidence of an actor accustomed to gracing the biggest stages on the planet—I walk over to the older officer and take him by the arm.

"I'm the nephew of the director of Bambino Gesù. I don't want any trouble, but those guys are a menace. They almost killed me. They must be on drugs."

The policeman doesn't ask me for any papers. He doesn't doubt my words for a moment. He starts looking at the three guys with their ripped jeans and shaved heads. In his mind, it's case closed. "We'll take care of it, don't worry, sir."

I leave the three guys in the hands of the Force. They're deathly white, wearing the classic expression of those with something to fear. The police have made them drop their trousers. They're searching them from head to toe. Unseen, I wave to them, then blow them a kiss.

This Tuesday night, we've got to give the Lactarium a once-over, one of the easiest jobs. If it's done right, you can finish by four. Usually, when we end work early, three of the team leave and the fourth—in rotation—stays until six to punch everyone's timecards.

I have my first coffee with Stefano. He's finished his shift and is ready to go home to his girlfriend. I try to steer the conversation several times. I'd like to tell him: "My dear Stefano, I want to ask you, as someone with a drinking problem, why you don't try cutting down on heroin? Alcohol also kills you, but with more restraint. You're wasting away too conspicuously. Why don't you try my way? You can shoot a gram on Friday evenings, on Saturdays too if you like, but lay off it during the week." But I don't have the courage to lecture him. Perhaps I would, if I could somehow present him with my own shining example, me of all people.

Stefano heads off. Just as I'm leaving the café, Giovanni's big hand shoves me back in.

"Where are you off to? The first one is on you today." Claudio and Luciano are standing behind him.

I've learnt about many illnesses over the course of these two months, not from textbooks or school, but here at the hospital, from the stories of sleepless fathers during endless nights. Others from nurses who illustrate them like films seen in the cinema, or from words stolen in lifts, stolen everywhere.

My knowledge isn't limited to illnesses. I can place at least two hundred faces of parents inside the hospital. Those of Salviati, Spellman, Sant'Onofrio, and Pio XII. I also recall many of their children, though not others, all those confined to their bed or unable to leave their ward for obvious reasons. Of course, in order to establish this silent acquaintance between us, certain conditions are required. The first concerns their stay. I'd say they have to remain here at least a good couple of weeks for me to commit them to memory.

One of the latest to enter my personal album is a woman no more than thirty years old, small in stature, her hair tied in a messy bun: she took much less time to etch herself on my memory. She permanently stands at the entrance to Pio XII, often accompanied by other people, often alone. Her delicate face seems contorted as if there's something pushing from within, wanting to come out of her eyes, her nose, every hole in her body.

The Lactarium has an endless array of fridges, steel counters on each side, and, naturally, baby bottles and breast pumps crammed everywhere. Since the work isn't too heavy, it lightens the mind, raising everyone's spirits. Luciano is still our favorite subject. Giovanni is giving him an impassioned lecture.

"You've got to talk to him. You've got to tell him, 'Uncle, I can't live how you lived. I'm not a priest, I like women.'"

"Fat ones," Claudio stresses.

Giovanni shushes him with a gesture.

"What's that got to do with it. He likes them the way he likes them. You've got to have it out with your uncle. Sooner or later, you're going to take it out on one of us, that's what worries me. I'm starting to get scared when I bend over." I envy Giovanni's ability to stay dead serious during his jokes. On more than one occasion, they've made me double over with laughter.

Outside the Lactarium, there's a scurry of nurses, then of parents appearing from the rooms. Claudio goes to the glass door and opens it. From the windows overlooking the entrance to Pio XII comes a frenzy of shouting, overlapping voices, crying children. We immediately run to the windows to look.

Amidst a cluster of people trying to calm her down, there she is, the girl who has just entered the album of my silent acquaintances. She seems possessed by the devil. A terrible force has descended on her delicate frame. Two or three men are trying to placate her, but she repels them like they were made of paper. Even her tongue is spelling out a dark, threatening alphabet. There's no demon inside her, just an irrepressible pain that's turned her into a Fury. All around are people summoned to that spectacle of pain, frozen to the spot. The girl has received some news, something that's made her explode like this. There's no other explanation.

"Let's go," Giovanni calls us to order.

We resume the once-over of the Lactarium without the amusement of minutes earlier; pain—no matter how immune someone professes to be—is a disease that infects everyone, even those who claim not to suffer from it.

By one o'clock, we've finished the first part of the once-over. My teammates go off to eat and I start my usual patrol. I now have a series of precise stops. There's the nurse at Salviati and the one at Spellman. I often mention Luciano, but now I too belong to the category of the necessarily celibate. My stroll ends at the entrance gate by the clinics, so my thoughts naturally turn to her. Over the last two months, I must've passed her at least twenty times. The madonna is looking ever more beautiful. She's changed her haircut, wearing it slightly longer now. I've regained a little confidence since working at the hospital. I'm still a timid wimp, but I want to talk to her at some point. Maybe I'll buy her a coffee, like adults do. I'll tell her about my writing. I've never given poems to a girl; she might be the first.

On the way back to the Lactarium, I pass the entrance to Pio XII. It's one-thirty, but the girl is still sitting on her bench. Fury has been replaced by silence. Her puffy eyes are the only reminder of the explosion a few hours ago. There are two men in their seventies by her side. She stands in the middle, looking tiny, helpless, an animal ready to receive the final blow.

Below Sant'Onofrio, a reflex I can't shake draws my gaze to Knock-Knock's window. It must've been late April when he left the hospital. I would've liked to somehow say goodbye to him, but I didn't get the chance.

At two-fifty, the Lactarium is looking its best, ready to welcome mothers and newborns. We lazily head towards our lift, the service lift. As we descend to the ground floor, Claudio complains about the chicory sandwich his wife has made him— they're now at each other's throats by his account—sickeningly stuffed with garlic. To prove his point, he breathes half an inch from Luciano's mouth. The poor guy doesn't even have time to recover before he's met with a second breath from the same distance, this time from Giovanni, flavored with tuna and to-mato. The usual scene ensues: Luciano gets pissed off at the shit he has to deal with, then he gets a series of slaps and smacks all over, much to everyone's amusement.

The lift stops on the second floor. An auxiliary nurse enters with a stretcher, empty at first glance. Then, in the half-light of the lift, one part at a time, a small body emerges from the white sheet. Five men and a dead child in a lift. Just silence, silence, and nothing more. The auxiliary—a man in his sixties—looks at each of us in turn.

"What the fuck have you been eating?"

"It's these two assholes. They breathed all over me," Luciano says in his Sardinian-inflected Italian.

"Fuck the lot of you," the auxiliary replies, addressing the four of us.

Everyone—including me—starts laughing again. Meanwhile, I caress the sheet covering that son, a shroud that'll be washed and disinfected until it loses every trace of the body it now protects.

My thoughts turn to the young woman who burst out of Pio XII tonight. Who knows, perhaps this child was hers, the one that had grown in her belly.

We reach the ground floor. The auxiliary continues with his cargo towards the little house for dead children. We head the other way, towards our changing room. Far away, before that green door, the girl-turned-Fury appears, coming towards her creature one step at a time, her arms outstretched, no more tears or shrieks.

As my eyes bid farewell to that mother and son for the last time, a flood streams from deep within me, an invisible fire that takes—word by word—the form of a prayer.

14

I bought a new mobile phone with my first pay check. A yellow one. I thought a flashy color like that would make it harder to leave on some bar counter, despite my forgetfulness.

Giovanni calls me at five on Wednesday afternoon.

"You need to come early tonight, no later than seven. The area manager is waiting for us. We've got to do something outside the hospital." I know him all too well now, him and his fits of rage.

I take this phone call as a blessing. At home, I can't deny myself sadness. The changes that Bambino Gesù has wrought in my life stop at the front door. It's a kind of order, a sequence of feelings, a journey that always leads to the same non-place. Here, I've no answer but the alcohol I crave.

Virgilio is the cooperative's area manager; Bambino Gesù is just one of the contracts he oversees. Despite his lofty name, Virgilio is a former laborer with a balding head and gangster's face.

He's the only area manager I know. My mental image of him was pretty much this, confirmed by the blazer he's sporting, squeezed tight over his paunch: the kind of guy who'd eat from his mother's skull to work his way up the cooperative. Anything to get the smell of wax remover and bleach off his hands.

"Guys, I talked to the cooperative director." He says it like it's some kind of royal charter, complete with a stamp and wax seal. "He personally promised it to a senior prelate, so it's a big deal."

Giovanni, already visibly irritated, emits a series of snorts.

"We've got to clear out some offices by the day after tomorrow. Naturally, you'll all get overtime."

"'We've got to,' Virge? Are you giving us a hand too?"

Virgilio flashes a fake smile at Giovanni's quip.

"Same old Gio. I'm not, no, but I told Massimo to give you a hand."

No sooner is he named than Massimo arrives with his rolling gait, already looking sharp in his uniform. He glances at us in turn; when he gets to Giovanni, he loses a bit of his polish.

"That's it?" Giovanni asks Virgilio. He nods.

"Yeah, that's it. You should be pleased. The less there are of you, the more overtime you get."

"Yeah, but we've only got one back, and when it breaks, it breaks."

Giovanni sets off, biting his tongue. We all follow in single file. Massimo comes up to me.

"Do we know anything more specific? Like how big this place is we've got to clear out and if we'll get any tools to use?" His voice betrays all his reluctance to get involved. I give him a shove in reply.

"Man up, Max, we're moving stuff, not going to war."

We drive the cooperative van into the center of Rome. The building we have to empty is at the start of Via del Corso. We're all fairly elated. We've got work to do, but it's better to do it on one of the world's most beautiful streets—bustling at all times of day and night with Italian and foreign girls—than to toil in a random suburb. Right in front of the building in question, a no parking area has been marked with red tape. The people in charge must've made arrangements with Rome City Council.

"Look at that. We've even got a place to park right in front."

Our elation ends at the building's double front door, the kind you usually see at a bank entrance with curved doors and bulletproof glass. Inside, there's just one immense room, ten thousand square feet at the very least, completely overflowing with desks and chairs, not to mention all the usual paraphernalia, including computers and filing cabinets.

A distinguished gentleman comes over to us, looking us up and down.

"Are you the movers?"

We nod like five trained dogs.

"When are your colleagues joining you?"

"It's just us, actually." Giovanni struggles to answer in standard Italian.

"Ah." The distinguished gentleman says nothing more. A loud honk sounds from outside. "The truck is here. You need to put everything in there. If that van is yours, please remove it immediately. That space is for the HGV."

"I knew it was too good to be true." Giovanni tosses the van keys to Luciano, who immediately dashes outside.

"Let's go and see what fate has in store for us."

Giovanni's comment fills everyone with optimism.

At first inspection, we come up with the following figures: one hundred and eighty-six desks, two hundred and forty chairs, one hundred and thirty computers, sixty-six filing cabinets.

"Come on. The sooner we start, the sooner we finish." Massimo goes over to one side of a desk. "Come on, Dan." He points to the other side.

The desks aren't too heavy. We soon reach the security door at the entrance. The opening must be around thirty inches wide, but the desks are nearer thirty-five, all exactly the same type and size.

"We'll have to take them apart one by one," says Giovanni.

All four of us bend down. The top is attached to the leg frame with four bolts, each of which have been subsequently soldered to secure them, making it practically impossible to disassemble.

We take a look under another desk and do the same check with the same result.

"Excuse me. Are all the desks soldered?" Giovanni asks the distinguished gentleman, who has been having a hushed exchange with the truck driver.

"Yes, it was a second-hand batch and they were all rickety. That was the only option."

"And how do you expect us to get a three-foot desk through a two-foot door?" From his reversion to Roman dialect, I deduce that Giovanni can no longer contain himself.

"The same way the men who brought them in did. They turned them upright and gradually took them through."

"Pardon me asking, but how long did it take to bring them in?"

The gentleman does a quick mental count. "Around a fortnight, give or take a day."

"What about the chairs and computers?"

"Well, I'd say it took around a month for us to get operational." Giovanni turns towards us, his eyes erupting with anger, then faces the gentleman again.

"And we're supposed to empty the whole lot in a night?"

"No, who told you that? The truck has a parking permit until five tomorrow evening."

Giovanni turns around and strides towards the exit.

"I'm going to talk to that son of a bitch Virgilio. Don't touch a thing."

Massimo, Claudio, and I obey the order. In the meantime, Luciano returns from the lobby.

"It's impossible to find parking around here. I got massively lucky." No one replies, so he takes a closer look at us. "So, what's the deal?"

"A big fucking deal. We're going to die here."

Giovanni returns right after. I've seen him angry plenty of times, but never like this.

"It's simple, either we do it or they kick us off the team. We each have to face facts and decide what to do." Giovanni is fully aware that none of us has a choice.

"Well, I'm the biggest fuckwit here. I'm not even on the team." Massimo wants to cry.

All five of us approach the double bulletproof door with a desk in order to come up with a system, to work out the best technique to get it through to the other side. Eventually, after about twenty minutes of trial and error, we realize that the only solution is to set it at an angle, slide part of it through, then position it vertically, and finally angle it again. And those desks really weigh something. During that absurd rotation, it's all too easy to trap your hands between a desk and the bulletproof doors.

It's half past nine in the evening. We split into the usual pairs: Giovanni with Claudio and me with Luciano; Massimo, alone, will handle the chairs and computers.

The first to leave traces of skin on the bulletproof door is me, moving desk number six. Our job isn't only to get them through that double-glazed, sheet-metal passage, but also to carry them to the truck, to wait for the driver to lift them up with the electric platform, and then to neatly load them into the belly of the HGV. The driver is also worried. He's a taciturn man from Molise. He's done the math to calculate whether he can fit everything in, and the result is far from certain.

My graze is followed by Claudio's, then it's Giovanni's turn, then back to me. Finally, Luciano closes the loop. Every desk requires us to perform a contortionist's act that places ever more weight on our hands, our arms. First diagonal, then vertical, then diagonal again. These words become our litany.

The distinguished gentleman carefully monitors the proceedings.

"Look, for this job we get an artistic director," Claudio said at one point. The gentleman heard but pretended not to. He's gone to the café opposite a couple of times, but he's never once offered us a thing, not even a coffee.

We take our first break at two. Giovanni has sprawled out on one of the countless goddamned desks we've still got to move. We make a quick calculation. We've taken out thirty-five. My colleagues eat in silence with the truck driver. I go out onto Via del Corso. It's a beautiful evening. The heat is acceptable, tempered by a light breeze. Life on Via del Corso has dwindled, but not ceased. A few foreigners are still wandering around, mingling with groups of men who have spilled out of some club.

We resume work at half two. My arms have had half an hour of rest, but the feeling lasts no time at all. It's already completely vanished by the second desk.

"Let's each take turns to do half-hour shifts moving the computers, then we can recover a little." Luciano is the first to ask to switch.

I end up paired with Massimo. From the very first desk, I realize his arms aren't strong enough to work comfortably. We get to the door and the desk slips out of his hand. He tries to laugh it off, but no one—myself included—is in a joking mood.

"To hell with them. To hell with the lot of them."

Now and then, Giovanni spews out half-sentences, snippets of thought or profanities. The distinguished gentleman has gradually withdrawn. Now he's reclining in an armchair, never taking his eyes off us.

At four o'clock, halfway through the bulletproof door, the top of a desk slips out of my hand. I try to catch it mid-air but fail. My left thumb gets crushed in the attempt. The edge of the desk has cut me. Nothing serious, but I need disinfectant and a bandage. The distinguished gentleman springs into action, returning with a bottle of alcohol from a cleaning trolley, but nothing resembling a bandage. I solve the problem with tape: I wrap a tissue around my hand and tape it up.

As we're loading yet another desk, there's a thud from the

entrance area. We rush over to take a look. Claudio is now in my place. The desk has slipped from his hands and he's massaging his wrist in pain. He's sweaty, tired.

"Don't look at me! Go away! Go away or I'll take it out on you!"

His voice has been replaced by an incensed hiss. He's furious with the distinguished gentleman, who has rushed to the door to find out the reason for the bang, perhaps to give him a hand.

At five, we task Massimo with finding an open café, telling him to get them to make thirty odd coffees and to pour them into a large bottle, then to bring some food, anything. We recount the desks. We've done eighty-five. Most of the computers and chairs are still inside. As we smoke in silence, I get a better look at my three teammates. They're all shattered. It's impossible to rank them. In all the time I've known them, I've never felt so close to them as I do now. What we've been assigned isn't a job, at least not in the recent sense of the word. You have to go back centuries—perhaps to the days of slavery—to call it that.

Massimo returns with a one-and-a-half-liter plastic bottle filled to the brim with coffee, and two paper bags, a dozen croissants in each. We devour the lot in five minutes, making two rounds with the coffee in large plastic cups. The distinguished gentleman tentatively approached us, perhaps hoping to be offered something. Giovanni, to spell out the situation, placed the coffee and croissants beside him and stared the man straight in the eye. The distinguished gentleman immediately retreated.

At ten to six, the agony resumes. I've never hated an inanimate object as much as those desks. I repeatedly wish them dead, but—luckily for them—they can't die. By the second desk, I remove the tape and tissue around my hand. I can't work freely with that compress. It only takes a few movements for the cut to start bleeding again. The result is a nice red stamp on every desk I touch. This cheers me up. They'll take something of me with them. Someone will be forced to wipe them with a disgusted look when they realize it's blood. Meanwhile, day has dawned on Via del Corso and life has returned to its brisk pace, along with the inevitable traffic.

When we re-count the desks, a wave of joy restores my strength a little. It's ten o'clock. One hundred and thirty-six desks down, exactly fifty to go.

"I've got to eat something." Giovanni's eyes are glazed over. He looks feverish.

"Savory, though," adds Claudio.

This time it's Luciano's turn. Everyone hands him ten thousand liras. He'll decide what to get, but the preference is for white pizza and various salamis. While we await his return, all four of us focus on the chairs and computers. Compared to the desk ordeal, it's a walk in the park. We put one chair on top of another. They're the ones with wheels; they basically carry themselves.

"Take a look at this, guys." We turn to Massimo, who proudly points to his invention: he's stacked not two, but three chairs on top of each other, placing a computer on the seat of the last chair. With one finger, he transports the contraption to the curved double entrance door. "Piece of cake." He caps this off with a smirk.

It really is a piece of cake. In the half hour we spend waiting for Luciano, we halve the number of chairs and computers that need loading.

Luciano returns, and the scent of mortadella wafts through the building. He has two loaded bags: one is full of white pizza, the other holds various waxed paper bundles. Sitting in a circle on the carpet, we eat in silence.

"Gio, is this worse than the once-over of that building in the EUR district?"

"No comparison. This is worse than everything," Giovanni replies with his mouth full.

At exactly twelve-forty, Luciano and I get the last desk through the door.

When we're outside, we embrace. The others arrive and also embrace us. Now it's time for the chairs and computers, but the worst is behind us. In spite of the raging fatigue, a little cheerfulness returns, aided by the incessant throng on Via del Corso.

Leaning against the truck, now overloaded with desks, we take a cigarette break. Our eyes follow the females in that stream of humans passing a yard away from us. Tall, short, blond, and dark, wrapped in office dresses or casual in flip-flops and shorts. Luciano doesn't miss a single girl. Happiness quickly turns to gloom.

"Come on, we better go." In the end, he's the one who marshals us, not because he wants to get back to work, but just to remove himself from the spectacle of all those women's bodies.

At four, we load the last computer into the truck. There are sounds of cracking plastic as we jam it in. The driver from Molise congratulates us. We've managed to squeeze everything in. He's never seen a job like that done in so little time.

The distinguished gentleman shakes our hands, one by one. "I'll be sure to tell the cardinal to speak to your managers. You've been truly outstanding." But none of us really cares.

We reach our van one step at a time. Now that the adrenalin is wearing off, I can start to feel all the aches and pains caused by the exertion. My hands in particular feel almost frozen. We no longer have the energy to speak. Even Massimo, who'd crack a joke at death's door, stays silent, his eyes half-closed.

We arrive at Bambino Gesù. On the short journey, both Giovanni and Claudio have fallen asleep. Massimo and I smoke, while Luciano drives.

Seeing us like this, the colleagues we encounter are speechless. Outside our office, we describe what they made us do. The comments immediately grow angry.

"Bastards, only bastards would make someone work for eighteen hours." Adriana, as a mother, is the most disgusted.

"What's that bitch Marianna doing?" asks Raffaella, a colleague who works in the wards.

"What's she doing?" Adriana replies. "She's sweating blood to get hired as an auxiliary at the hospital, that's what. Would you rather work for a cooperative or get a job at Bambino Gesù, maybe even at the Vatican?"

Fabio arrives from the corridor accompanied by Celso. They turn serious as soon as they see us.

"We got back alive, unfortunately. Tell Virgilio if he wanted to kill us, it failed." Giovanni seems on the verge of exploding.

"I knew nothing about it, Gio. I swear on my daughter." Fabio replies and no one can doubt his sincerity.

"We'll talk about what they made you do, I promise, but there's something else now: Celso has come to say goodbye. This morning, he gave in his resignation at headquarters."

Celso—summoned—smiles with embarrassment.

"Yeah, I've found work in Priverno. My printer job."

Everyone gives him an affectionate send-off.

"Best of luck," I tell him, after an embrace. I'd like to talk to him, wishing him all the happiness that life has denied him so far, but I've neither the strength, nor the time. Celso departs and a sudden, unmanageable nostalgia drains what little energy I had left. I wonder if I'll ever see him again, how he'll continue his life, if he'll ever be able to forget the hospital where his son stayed forever. Good luck forever, dear Celso.

You could hear a pin drop in the changing room. Our afternoon colleagues have heard about our adventure and have come to say hello. They're silent too.

"You look like a zombie," Stefano says, gently tugging my ear. Then they leave us alone. We start to slowly get changed. My uniform has barely dried from all the sweat I've poured into it. The hardest challenge is unbuttoning my polo shirt. My fingers hardly respond.

The sob takes everyone by surprise.

"Sorry," Giovanni says, when his crying has become unstoppable. We stand there, unsure what to do. He weeps facing the wall, hunched over. "It's just I can't tie my shoes. I can't close my hands anymore."

Luciano is the first to act. "Don't worry Gio, it's nothing." He ties them up for him.

Giovanni finishes changing without another glance at us.

"I'm taking a sick day tomorrow," he says as he's about to leave.

Massimo and I—along with Luciano and Claudio—say goodbye at the entrance to the ER. Giovanni's sobs have remained in our ears, in our hearts. Now no one can say which is stronger, tiredness or sorrow.

15

T hey've destroyed you."
When my mother wants to be melodramatic, she does so masterfully, holding my injured hand between her own, then examining the other. I have at least a dozen cuts, not counting the bruises on my skin.

It's been a long time since I've seen her like this, with no feeling other than concern, the animal urge to defend a son desecrated by someone beyond the hearth. I've become used to seeing her defeated, gripped by impotent despair, with nothing to do but be present for a son who suffers too much from living, to the point of wanting to lose himself, fully succeeding.

This time, even I'm surprised. On the way home, I thought I'd fall asleep the moment I laid my body on the bed, but I don't. Though besieged by pain, physically exhausted, I begin my mad ricochet in search of sleep. It's nerves. They've supported me through the many hours of shifting desks and have no intention of relenting now. Far from it; the more they work, the more fired up they get.

At eight in the evening, my father comes to greet me. I can see something forgotten on his face, lost behind the years. My father can't resist giving me a caress, fleeting, already over.

"We should've got you to help with the removal. It would've taken us half as long."

My father smiles at me. His face carries me off to sleep with the sweetness of when everything was still intact, as a child.

It's after three in the afternoon when my mother comes to wake me. I've slept for nineteen hours straight and God knows how many more would've passed if she hadn't been there. I swallow a painkiller with the mug of coffee. My arms feel heavy as lead. All the cuts and scratches on my hands are taut, ready to immediately open up again as soon as I try some more demanding movements.

Even driving is a strain, especially on my arms, but I eventually make it to the hospital. I've already got everything planned for my after-work recreation. Some quiet drinking in the Castelli Romani area. I'm in too bad a shape to go to unknown spots; it's better to play at home. Some bar in Albano will do just fine.

I clock in at four-forty. Antonio is there. Instead of ageing, he gains weight, slowly but surely.

"Claudio and Giovanni are off sick. Virgilio just called. He said you all did a great job. You and Luciano can skip the regular once-over of the blood collection center tonight. You can just do all the easy jobs."

Luciano arrives. He's a mess too, looking skinnier than usual. His thick glasses seem even bigger on his long, narrow face.

"It's just us. No once-over," I tell him as he joins me.

"Too right. My uncle had to splash my face with cold water to get me out of bed."

We find Carmelo in the changing room.

"Hey guys, I heard about the bloodbath. Fuck them."

We nod. I feel a bit like a returning veteran. I'm gratified by all this attention.

"Of course, some people in this cooperative are treated like dirt and others do as they please. Amir went to Egypt and he's coming back in two weeks. He says his mother is dying. Stefano didn't show up. He's probably doped up at home."

Luciano and I stop by the café. We both go for a double espresso in a large cup.

"We were meant to go out tonight, but where can we go in our state? Straight to a hospice."

I'd completely forgotten about the promise I'd made him, that for once we'd postpone going out together for a genuine reason, rather than with an excuse, as we've done a thousand times before. "Ah yeah, shame."

Luciano, after a few moments of resignation, perks up again in response to something that's going through his mind.

"Why don't we save it for tomorrow. Saturday. The perfect day, right? We've got over a day to recover. What do you reckon? Are you up for it?"

"I reckon that's perfect. Let's do it tomorrow night then." I really don't know what else to say.

After coffee, at a snail's pace, we head for the office. My brain is working out the various alternatives to offer Luciano. I don't know exactly what he's expecting. I haven't been to the cinema for at least two years. Maybe he'd enjoy a good film. The thing that scares me most is how to deal with my situation. I'm not supposed to drink at all and it irritates me. Maybe he's a drinker too. Not like me of course, but who'd turn down a nice beer?

Knock knock.

My eyes move to his window, but there's no one there. It really sounded like him, though. Luciano has also stopped. He looks at me blankly.

"Go on. I'll be right there," I tell him. I go back to the window, but it's deserted. Maybe it was just an ordinary *knock knock*.

Knock knock.

My eyes search, racing from floor to floor.

Knock knock.

They eventually find him, on the top floor, last window.

When we're sure each of us is watching the other, we wave. Knock-Knock seems unchanged. He may have lost a little weight, but his smile and eyes are still the same. We stay like that, staring at each other from afar. I don't know how much time passes. Then he rests his horned hand on the window. I discreetly reciprocate, trying to spell out to him, word by word, "What's your name?" I can't keep calling him Knock-Knock, even if I've grown fond of this nickname. But he can't understand my sentence. In the end, I wave him goodbye. Whenever I do this, his face darkens. He never waves back. He leaves the window and that's it.

I arrive at the office thinking of Knock-Knock, of the happiness I felt at seeing him again, a selfish and inexcusable feeling: I should wish to never see that child again. It would mean that his need for medical treatment is over, that he's permanently restored to health.

"So, here's the plan. Luci, you go to the orthopedic ward since Nadia is off. Just give it a dusting and empty the bins, that's all. Dan, go and give the floor a clean in the anatomical pathology laboratory. Same thing. A quick going-over and you're done."

I'd heard about it, but never had to work there. Luciano immediately turns to me.

"Dan, the less you look up the better. Everyone has cleaned it at some point." I'd hoped he was going to suggest swapping jobs, but I can see it in his face: he's afraid of that place too.

The anatomical pathology laboratory has various rooms. I only have to set foot in the first ones—which have nothing frightening about them—and I'm assailed by anxiety that's almost impossible to swallow.

There are still a couple of workers in the offices. A few minutes after my arrival, they turn off their computers and leave. It's six-thirty on a Friday afternoon. The week is over for them.

At the end of the corridor, there's a large door with tinted glass panes. My colleagues talk about what lies beyond like it's

a horror film. The tale is even more effective when told to colleagues who are new to the hospital, giving everyone the satisfaction of seeing the disgust on their faces turn to ever-growing
fear.

I clean the offices in less than half an hour, absorbing myself
with trivial chores just to stall for time, to find the right moment
to walk through the door that'll take me to the main room.

My preparation makes me look like a free diver. I suck in air,
fill my lungs to the max as if there were no oxygen inside, check
to make sure all the light switches are on, and enter.

As I approach the first two shelves, Luciano's words echo
in my head: "Dan, the less you look up the better." I try to
concentrate on the grouting between the individual floor tiles.
Even at our house, they're not that white. You can only see this
level of cleanliness at Bambino Gesù. But no matter how hard I
try to focus elsewhere, my eyes wander off on their own. A second's glance is enough for me to immediately lower them. I try
to fill my mind with my favorite poems: "My soul, make haste.
I'll lend you my bicycle, but hurry. And with people, please be
careful, don't pause to talk and stop pedaling."

But not even Caproni's verses can transport me away from
this place.

I reach the central room. There's a steel table in the middle
and counters all around, also made of steel. On top, there are
more jars, countless, all transparent, all full. I fill the bucket
with water, then it's time for bleach. Cleaning the floor is obviously easy enough since my eyes are where they should be. The
room isn't very big. It doesn't take me more than thirty minutes
to clean it at half speed. Now it's dusting time.

Everything that upsets me always has the same root cause.
It doesn't matter whether it's an autopsy room for children or a
sunset with haunting colors. These are just part of the stage design. The container varies, but the question that dances within
it never changes. Who determines events? Why do I have to

witness—floating in glass jars—pieces of a child, some unrecognizable, others as dreadfully familiar as an arm, a hand, a foot?

If you, God, are behind everything, why didn't you take me? Or any other adult on the face of the earth? People with years behind them, who have rejoiced and suffered, who have given and taken. While this hospital casts a shadow for me to chase every day, it also annihilates me with the indecipherable fate of countless children. And I'm incapable of appealing to faith. If it's you, God, behind everything, what you're doing here isn't right. You—not us—should ask for forgiveness.

When I finish cleaning, my legs are shaking. Exhaustion has descended on me even more forcefully than yesterday. As I walk to the office—hunched over, wearing my third pair of worn-out sneakers, both with the soles detached at the toe—I run into her.

Today, the madonna is wearing a light floral dress and a pale blue cardigan that matches the color of her eyes. Courage consists of moments, instants that become decisive. I approach her without a doubt in my mind. My eyes have seen too much atrocity inside jars drowning in formalin.

"Excuse me."

My courage automatically vanishes the moment I open my mouth. She stops, smiling. Up close, she's beautiful enough to be the envy of almost all the female sex.

"Sure, go ahead."

Now the difficult—actually, insurmountable—part.

"I . . . I wanted to tell you that you're pretty, really pretty."

The madonna smiles.

"Thanks."

It's the greatest gift life has ever given me.

"In the last few months, we've often passed each other. I wanted to tell you."

"Thanks."

She doesn't seem to have other words in her vocabulary. She resumes walking one step at a time. I stay by her side.

"I'd like to buy you coffee sometime. I work for the cooperative. I also write, I've been publ—"

"What?"

"I said I've been published."

"No, what you said before."

"Coffee. If you want, I'd like to buy you one sometime."

The madonna starts walking quickly again. She has a surprised, certainly not positive expression.

"Wait." At my request, she stops again, making no effort to appear less annoyed than she is. "These last few months we seemed to often make eye contact. I thought you'd like that too."

"Often make eye contact?"

"Yes."

The smile that appears on her face hurts more than all the hours of moving furniture the other night. "I'm sorry, but this is the first time I've seen you."

My masochism gene thrives in these situations.

"Fair enough. Well, now you see me. The coffee offer still stands."

The madonna looks up to the heavens. When her eyes return to my face there's nothing angelic about her, although she's still beautiful, gorgeous.

"I'll spell it out for you. No. And don't pester me anymore. I'm a lawyer. I work for the hospital's legal department. Have I made myself clear?"

The meaning of her words is unequivocal, but I want to hear her tell me.

"Don't lawyers drink coffee?"

Now the madonna smiles demonically.

"Of course, but not with workers from the cooperative." Then she turns and leaves. My masochism is sated. I stay perfectly still, riveted to the spot.

As I walk towards the office, more than once I'm on the verge of chasing after that girl. Certainly not to repeat my invitation. I'd just like to tell her that her worldview is lacking, very lacking.

In these months, I've learnt that there's no role, birth, or affiliation that can represent a human being in their entirety. Some of my colleagues have so much acumen and strength that they'd be the envy of all those who—through unfathomable quirks of fate—were simply born luckier, in places where even their mediocrity was enough to open doors for them, opportunities unthinkable to those who haven't had the same good fortune. I'd also tell her that eyes are for looking, that she's protecting the interests of a hospital she doesn't understand. You only have to spend a day exploring it to witness the annihilation of the social classes to which she so faithfully appealed. I'm not offended, but I do feel sorry for her.

I arrive at the office with tremendous serenity. The girl of my dreams has just called me a failure, yet I feel fine, not even the slightest bit hurt by her words.

I find myself facing a cluster of colleagues. Virgilio stands on the step leading to our office. The atmosphere isn't great. I struggle to understand. Then Luciano comes towards me. He's not wearing his glasses.

"Stefano is dead." His eyes well up as soon as he says it.

"What do you mean, dead?"

"Last night. He hit a traffic light on his moped."

I've received this news on other occasions. The stunned feeling is always the same: a disbelief that strips away the substance of logic, a fact you instinctively can't accept. Then a hot flush. Stefano's face as he calls me a zombie, just yesterday, and all the words spoken, the casual bullshit. His slender body wandering the boulevards. Putting on his uniform. Talking to me about flowers and the future.

Stefano is dead, gone, finished. I'll never see him again in this life.

I sit away from the others on a step. For once, I don't have to hide to cry, like I always do. The entrance to our office is packed. There's no corner that isn't occupied by a colleague. The most desperate is Carmelo. His round face is flushed. Besides the pain, he must be feeling that way out of guilt, though everyone—at least once—mouthed off about Stefano. Even me with the life I lead.

Virgilio joins me, asking Luciano to come closer. He too has been affected by the news. His lips are dry, chapped.

"You two are done for the night. Go and get some rest. Thanks for the removal. And tell that to Claudio and that stubborn ass Giovanni on Monday."

It's nine. As Virgilio suggested, Luciano and I leave without punching our timecards. At headquarters, he'll put us down as being present until midnight.

Most of my colleagues have gone. Apart from Luciano and me, only Antonio has remained to give the tool-room keys to the women working in the wards.

The news about Stefano was revived every time it was pronounced. From face to face, surprise after surprise. Even for those of us who had already received it, it kept returning to our throats.

"Dan, what do you reckon, shall we postpone tomorrow as well? Shall we go out next week?"

"No." I answer Luciano with stony resolve. "If Stefano was here, he'd tell us to go and have fun. Anyway Luci, don't you see? Life is all just madness. Actually, we should hang out for Stefano's sake."

"You're right, Dan."

Luciano and I go our separate ways with a plan to meet here at the Janiculum at eight tomorrow evening.

As I drive, Stefano appears before me at every street corner. Him, his voice, terrible visions of what must be left of him.

Still. From an inner place that's not my brain. Still I find myself praying as the only possible reaction, whether sensible or senseless, or out of terror in the face of our furthest limit, newly demonstrated. Whatever the reason, it doesn't matter.

When you're torn from the fog of the ordinary, when war explodes close to you, then all that's left is this word launched towards the stars.

Keep him warm. Content. Freed from everything.

"A glass of white." Tonight, I'll repeat this magic formula ad infinitum. Here's the first flowing in my flesh. Fresh nectar that softens everything in existence. Never have I awaited forgetfulness as eagerly as tonight. May it be the greatest ever.

16

Remember nothing."
Since last night, I've obeyed this command and nothing else.

Lately, forgetfulness has been playing hard to get. Perhaps because work has got my body back in shape. Perhaps because there's less alcohol in my bloodstream due to the intermittent abstinence during the week. But all it takes is to pick up the pace, to make more frequent stops, and problem solved.

There's almost nothing of the last few hours in my memory.

My mother trying everything to stop me going out, a little girl clinging to my leg all the way to the front door.

Nothing else.

It's seven-fifty when I arrive at the Janiculum. Despite my drunken state, I'm still a respectful guy. Luciano has already arrived, but he hasn't seen me. He's wearing a red polo shirt. His hair is slicked back with gel. He's spruced up.

I stop an inch away and he jerks sideways in fright. I stretch over to open the door for him.

"There you go."

I try to pinpoint the reasons, to forcibly stop myself, but Luciano's entry into my car is met with a growing feeling of annoyance. It's so strong that I can't look him in the face, nor even talk to him. Annoyance turns to anger. I have to drink, and having this guy with me complicates things. Who is he? What does he want from me? Luciano is everything I can't be. A normal guy. Calm. Ready to enjoy the evening ahead of us.

Don't Close Your Eyes

17

Claudio bid us farewell on the thirty-first of July. He moved to San Giovanni Hospital to be closer to home. From Quarto Miglio, where he lives, it's basically strolling distance. Right from day one, there have been two versions of his departure from Bambino Gesù. One that he wanted to transfer, just as he claimed, and another spicier version that his dismissal came "from above" to appease a nun who had supposedly seen him kissing Cinzia in the underground corridors. The nun then spoke to the hospital director, who in turn called the cooperative's management. This second version is corroborated by a piece of evidence, which almost everyone agrees is conclusive. It just so happens that Cinzia also left, according to her because she was tired of being at Bambino Gesù; she now works at a government office near Garbatella. When we got back from holiday, news came of the definitive split between Claudio and his wife. Actually, she seems to have kicked him out of the house.

On the first of September, Massimo joined the team to replace Claudio. Giovanni swore about it for days, but in the end, as usual, he had to accept. Almost anyway. First, he delivered a knockout blow. He asked—demanded—to rotate the pairs. Luciano went with him. Everyone was happy with this new arrangement: Giovanni, who didn't have to pair up with Massimo—unsuitable for the team in his view—and me, since Massimo, over the past few months, has become the teammate I spend most time with. But most of all, Giovanni's request pleased Luciano.

Our relationship has become more complicated since our night out.

More than three months have passed and although he claims to have gotten over his anger, he still looks tense to me. Luciano hasn't forgiven me—and who knows if he ever will—for the night I put him through. A night from hell, by his own account. I obviously don't remember anything. On the Monday following our Saturday together he arrived at Bambino Gesù with his glasses broken in half, held together with yellow tape. He couldn't even look me in the eye. When I asked him to tell me exactly what had happened, he exploded and—filled with rage I'd never seen in him before—replied: "You're fucking kidding me, now you want me to tell you about it?"

Of course, I wasn't trying to make fun of him. I just wanted to know—given the profound forgetfulness of those hours—how events had unfolded. Just out of curiosity, that's all. I'd never had a companion witness what I usually do in my absence.

The events of that Saturday night went something like this.

After picking him up at the Janiculum, we headed for Lake Albano, one of my usual haunts, to have dinner at a little restaurant owned by some people I know. The dinner, washed down with a chilled bottle of Frascati white wine, was—according to him—the only enjoyable part. Then we returned to Rome. The first trill of horror—again, in his own words—came at the entrance to the Raccordo Anulare ring road from the Appian Way. I made a misguided attempt to overtake a bus, oblivious to the narrowing carriageway: it was only his intervention—he practically wrenched the steering wheel from my hands—that prevented us from sliding under the tip of the guard rail. After this scare—by his account—we drove to Trastevere, to a little bar with a name I couldn't remember. We sat on a small sofa right in front of the dance floor, where some girls were dancing together, gorgeous. On the third white, as I got up to take a piss, I passed out on the coffee table where he'd just put down his glasses, which instantly snapped in two.

But the best part, or worst part, happened outside the bar. At three, totally incapacitated, I said I'd like to go home. He told me I better not: I should sleep at his place, I couldn't drive in that condition. Every time Luciano tells this story—to practically every colleague—his expression from this point on changes from good-natured to serious, almost fearful: "When I told him to come and sleep at my place he went crazy, shouting at me that no one tells him what to do. Then he climbed on top of a car and started jumping from roof to roof. When people began to show up, saying 'call the police,' I took off."

Time, fortunately, has dulled the interest in our night out, but for weeks it was on every colleague's lips. I've always tried to downplay what happened by passing it off as an evening gone wrong, perhaps because of the squid we ate at the restaurant, which tasted of ammonia. I bought Luciano a new pair of glasses, as was only fair. Three hundred thousand liras from my May paycheck.

Up until the holidays, there were basically three topics of discussion between us cooperative workers. Claudio and Cinzia. My and Luciano's evening. Stefano.

As the days passed, a slow, unstoppable transformation took place. Stefano's death left us vulnerable, especially because of our sense of guilt over the rumor each of us had fueled regarding his condition. As soon as the pain became manageable, back came the moral judgments, the murderous assessments. Pretty much everyone backtracked. They no longer considered his death as a calamity to endure and nothing more. No, they all felt obliged to consign it to their memory as the end of a guy who ultimately deserved nothing more than to die that way.

Even I, at one point, felt compelled to judge his life.

A week or so after his death, the girl he was living with visited the hospital; the rumors had also constructed a clearly defined character for her: an incurable junkie like him, perhaps she was already dead too. Reality shattered that image at first sight. Fabio asked me to accompany her to our changing room so she could empty the locker that belonged to her boyfriend. Stefano's girlfriend was—is—stunning. Her innate gentleness had been torn by grief, but she still represented everything I wanted from life. No resemblance to a junkie. I didn't dare say anything to her. I accompanied her as Fabio had asked and stayed there with her for as long as necessary, glancing at her from time to time. I said goodbye to her at the hospital exit.

I stood watching her until she was out of sight.

Though I didn't say a word to her, at that very moment I felt pissed as hell at Stefano: with a love like that by his side, why did he need to torment his veins? My anger immediately vanished. After that single instant, Stefano's gentle smile reappeared, the one I carry and will continue to carry until my death.

This Wednesday night, the general medicine day hospital awaits us. One of the largest and shabbiest facilities. One of the once-overs we try our best to avoid.

I'm struggling to properly focus on work and the fact we've got a very laborious task ahead of us cheers me up: if nothing else, it'll allow me to disconnect from the anxiety that's been tormenting me for days.

Tomorrow evening, at nine, I'll take part in a poetry reading at an art gallery behind Piazza Navona. Many poets will be there and I haven't read in public for almost a year. My job has given me back the strength to interact with people, to spend time among others again, but standing in front of an audience that listens to you is another matter. Although I know I'll take a break from the weekday sobriety I've imposed on myself— since without a few whites it would be unthinkable to even try—my dread is almost unbearable. All it takes is the slightest lapse in concentration and I'm confronted with images of everything that could go wrong tomorrow night. Because that's all my mind anticipates.

A night of extreme exertion is just what's needed. At least my thoughts won't bark so loud.

To prepare as best we can for the once-over ahead of us, our team has decided to meet earlier. I get to the hospital at nine. Giovanni is already in the office with Fabio; Luciano and Massimo haven't arrived yet.

"Ready, Dan? We're going to have fun tonight."

"Never readier."

I now have a relationship of complete trust with Giovanni. That wild evening with Luciano aggravated him too, then it all blew over. Giovanni and I get on well because we share the same vision of work. It has to be done well, to the best of our ability, out of fairness to ourselves, first and foremost. I know almost everything about the others but next to nothing about him, aside from his passion for fishing. When you try to dig into his private life, Giovanni instinctively clams up, says little, and changes the subject. He lives alone, his parents are in a hamlet near Ladispoli, that's it. There are rumors he's having an affair with a woman at the hospital, but no one can confirm this. The lack of information has inevitably multiplied these rumors, these speculations about his life outside work. And rumors, without a trail to follow, always point to the worst: hidden vices, strange relationships, concealed secrets. I don't believe any of this. Giovanni's life—perhaps this is the real basis of our understanding—quite simply happens almost entirely in here, as does mine. What little lies beyond is a minor detail. In my case, it all revolves around emptying a glass; for him, it's fishing, rest, maybe desire for a woman who'll show up at some point.

Luciano and Massimo arrive almost simultaneously, each with their own cooler bag with dinner inside.

"I almost forgot, Dan. Look what's arrived." Fabio beckons

me into the office. There are some boxes of safety shoes beside his desk.

"Incredible." I start running my finger down the sizes: forty-two, forty-three, another forty-two, then forty-four.

"No forty?" I ask Fabio. He shrugs.

"I don't know what to tell you. There were some smaller sizes, but Marianna came by. She took three or four boxes for her colleagues who work in the wards."

"Naturally."

I stayed home for the August break. I had the money to plan a holiday, but no one to spend it with. So, I opted for the usual, inexpensive loneliness, free of all the false illusions that a holiday entails. Besides, I couldn't do it. I didn't have the courage. Nowadays I can do everything by myself, but not a whole holiday. The melancholy would overwhelm me, to the point of killing me, and I'd hate to die far from home.

My relationship with loneliness has worn thin, just as with everything else. There was a time when alcohol was still a pleasant soundtrack, when going out alone meant being with everyone, all the people I passed on the street. I had a wonderful inability to understand the concept of unknown, alien. I carry with me unforgettable encounters from that period: faces, stories as deep as the whole human adventure. Loneliness starts from within. It can mean being with the whole world or the exact opposite; feeling that you've enclosed yourself in a sarcophagus, nailed from inside. That's how I felt for a long time.

Then came the job, this hospital. In here—in an absurd, unjustified way—I feel part of everything. There's no distance between me and what lives around me, for better or for worse. I've rediscovered friendship at Bambino Gesù, the selflessness of gestures made for their own sake. My teammates have put their lives in my hands dozens of times and I've done the same for them. At Bambino Gesù, I've got to know pain taken to its purest essence, invincible. I've sworn. I've cursed this flesh that's unable to defend itself against others' pain, let alone seek to shun it. I carry tons of unwritten words on all this, left lying around in my mind, forgotten and reclaimed hundreds of times as reality continues to present them to me in their full magnitude. Yet, thanks to all this, I've come back to life a little each day.

Here it is. The general medicine day hospital will be renovated soon; it's the exception proving the rule that Bambino Gesù is a model for other hospitals. The waiting room has a greenish linoleum floor covered with patches. The whole surface is worn out. You can clean and wax all you want, but it is what it is. The walls are also linoleum, in the same greenish color. Less wear and tear has preserved a more vivid shade compared to the floor, but the contrast doesn't help. On the contrary, it makes the overall look of the central hall even more depressing. There's a series of felt-tip scribbles on the walls—resistant to all kinds of detergent, from degreasers to acids—mostly signed by a certain Dodo who decided to leave his autograph at least thirty times.

Despite it being late September, it's still sweltering, and the large waiting room is only air-conditioned on paper. Steering the scrubber-dryer—since these days no one can prize it from my hands—I set to work with Massimo beside me. Giovanni and Luciano have started to move desks and furnishings from the various doctors' offices, a dozen rooms opening onto two separate corridors.

"Cigarette, please," I say, without taking my eyes off the foam created by the scrubber-dryer's abrasive disc. Massimo slides the pack of MS out of my trouser pocket, pulls one out, sticks it in my mouth, and lights it. With the smoking cigarette in the corner of my mouth, I keep pushing as hard as I can to make that floor at least passable. The general medicine day hospital is on the first basement floor. One of the routes to get there is the connecting passage. It's still early, quarter to eleven, but as the light descends this underground passage feels eerie to anyone who's easily spooked. When I'm alone, I usually prefer to go via the outer avenues. All too often down there I've jumped in fright at some figure suddenly flying out one of the many doors along the way. Even now—clutching the scrubber-dryer and smoking a cigarette, surrounded by three other large grown men—I can't look at the tunnel without feeling a strange, unwarranted disquiet.

The more my eyes fear something before me, the more they constantly dart towards it. My umpteenth fleeting glance reveals a quick flash: a naked body right in the center of the passageway, about twenty yards from us. By the time I look back at it, everything has vanished. But I saw that body. I've hallucinated many times, especially in my raver days, even with alcohol when the delirium turns violent. I know how to distinguish between a projection and reality, however absurd. I immediately switch off the scrubber-dryer.

"What's the matter, Danny?" Massimo notices my consternation.

"I think I saw someone." I walk towards the tunnel, but first I turn to Massimo. "You come too, I'm scared to go alone."

Unnoticed by Giovanni and Luciano, we start to make our way down the tunnel, very cautiously, walking side by side.

"What did you see, exactly?" Massimo also lacks courage. The tone of his voice leaves no doubt about that.

"I saw someone, naked."

"How do you mean naked?" Massimo instantly stops.

"Naked, completely white."

We continue shoulder to shoulder for another twenty yards or so, then, between two empty laundry trolleys, we glimpse a figure with its face to the wall. It's naked, totally.

"That's the one."

We very slowly approach. The figure becomes more defined. He's a boy. He must be fourteen, fifteen at most. His body rhythmically sways.

"Excuse me," I try to say, but he doesn't react. "Excuse me." Nothing.

Now we're no more than two feet away from him. He certainly must've heard us, but our presence doesn't change his behavior one iota. He stays facing the wall, constantly rocking back and forth. Preceded by a terrible stench, streams of excrement and urine trickle down his inner thighs. Massimo and I exchange glances.

"This one must've come from a pavilion."

"The Ford."

With all the care in the world, I reach out a hand towards the boy's arm. Perhaps this contact will wake him from the state he's fallen into. My hope fades at once. I slowly turn him towards us. Outwardly, he's a normal boy, only his eyes warn of sickness, staring, fearful.

"Let's get you to your ward now, O.K.?"

He doesn't offer any resistance. It must've exhausted him to be moved away. He drags his feet. Only his rocking remains unchanged. This close up, the stench is overpowering. I turn my head the other way to breathe. Massimo walks three feet behind—we decided this together—so he can immediately step in if the boy tries anything. I've developed an amazing rapport with Massimo. Most of the time we don't even need a word. We talk to each other in glances, and we trust each other blindly, just as I'm doing now.

One thing about the boy we're accompanying strikes me most of all, and it has nothing to do with his illness. I've never seen such white skin. Once when I was camping, I met an albino, a really nice guy, but that's a whole other matter. This boy has pearly, shiny, shimmering skin. He seems made of living ceramic, a priceless rarity. Who knows how much attention he would've attracted without his sickness, how many female hands would've wanted to touch him.

Three nurses are standing outside the Ford, talking vociferously among themselves. One paces nervously back and forth, swearing between every sentence. Their agitation is due to the boy we're bringing back. His escape must've caused a good deal of trouble. They come towards us when they see us. The swearing male nurse gives me a delighted hug, effortlessly lifting me up.

"Cheers guys, you've saved our lives. Coffee is on me whenever you want." Then they take the moon-skinned boy.

"Are you trying to scare us to death, Paolino? You know you can't leave the ward." He lets them take him, just as he did with us.

As we walk towards the general medicine day hospital, I can't distract myself. I try to keep my mind focused on the work ahead, but it's no use. Now I know how I function. It'll take a little time, a few one-liners from Massimo or Giovanni, and little by little I'll be back among the living, until the moment it's all over.

"Bastards, you go off without a fucking word to us." Giovanni and Luciano stand in the middle of the day hospital waiting room, glowering at us.

"Yeah, we went dancing, then two smoking babes took us back to theirs." Massimo replies, miming a woman's curves with his hands. Luciano—whose judgment on this subject is getting ever more clouded—instantly takes the bait.

"Really?"

"Sure, we went dancing, picked some girls up, went back to their house and banged them. All in ten minutes. For fuck's sake, Luci, use your brain." Luciano realizes he's been had. "Some poor boy got out of the Ford and we brought him back in. Happy now?"

While Massimo ends the discussion, I get back to the

scrubber-dryer. It's eleven-thirty. The general medicine day hospital is a battle that's just begun.

At five, the once-over is complete and our satisfaction is pretty much zero. The day hospital doesn't look much different from how we found it last night.

"At least it's disinfected now," Massimo pipes up, but his observation doesn't lift anyone's spirits.

When we arrive at the office, there's already a swarm of colleagues getting ready for the morning. Marianna, the union rep, is there too. My eyes are drawn to the feet of her entourage, four or five female colleagues who never leave her side. Now they all have new shoes.

"Nice shoes," I tell them all, especially Marianna, but neither she nor the others dare to answer.

The sun is already up. Hands in my pockets, I walk towards the car.

Knock knock.

I don't doubt for a second that it's him.

He's been absent from the hospital since late June. He must've spent his holidays back home, wherever that is.

I search for him in the windows of his ward. I eventually find him in a different room than the other times.

Knock-Knock has gotten worse. There's no need for a clinical examination to work this out. The grey pajamas I've seen him wearing in the past are suddenly two sizes bigger. His face is also different. Less chubby, his eyes sunken into sharp cheekbones. Serious, as usual, he greets me. CUCK-OLD. He flashes his dazzling white smile.

My mind wanders to the moon-skin of that other defenseless boy we brought back to the Ford tonight.

CUCK-OLD, I reply. We stand still, watching each other. Time passes but neither he nor I move. It may be from tiredness, partly from the sun beating down on my head, but just standing there watching him rests my body and mind.

No nurse can keep me away, no spinelessness can stop me. I want to meet Knock-Knock. He has to tell me his name, where he comes from, why he spends these stints inside the hospital.

"Good morning, Director."

A nurse produces a very broad smile.

The stooped figure of the director hurries past me. It's six in the morning and he's already walking at his usual brisk pace, his face aimed at the ground.

When I look up again, Knock-Knock has gone. He must've been offended because I stopped watching him. I know him well by now.

18

T he reading. It was my last thought before falling asleep and my first when I woke up, after just four hours of sleep.

Trying to rationalize fear is as futile as attempting to downplay tonight's event. Comments like "What does it matter?" "Just enjoy it!" and "It's not like you're going to war!" only add to my irritation. I'm well-aware I'm not going to war, just as I'm aware that I could approach everything—I mean really everything—with much more serenity. The problem isn't awareness, but the ability to act on it.

"Sorry, but what's the worst that could happen? What are you scared of? That you get stuck? That you don't read well?"

My mother—coffee in hand—updates the list of useless questions I hear every time. Just like everyone else, she doesn't understand that the problem isn't what will happen during the reading, what may or may not work out. The real problem is getting to that point, spending hellish hours in anguish, endlessly living and reliving the same scene.

It's eleven in the morning. A rough measure of my pulse already puts my resting heart rate above a hundred. Average, sadly.

Extremely slowly—with the grain and then against it—I shave for the occasion. My father brought me up to see bearded men as slovenly, even dirty. You need to have two ultra-smooth cheeks, the scent of aftershave, a whole different thing.

I dress a little more carefully than usual, slipping on a polo shirt and a pair of freshly laundered jeans. From the wardrobe, now dusty from disuse, I pull out every self-respecting poet's toolkit. A bag—crumpled just the right amount—to store books, notebooks, and notes. I stuff mine with just five A4 sheets of poems I'd like to read. I find an old magazine inside with some of my unpublished pieces, plus other sheets covered with my handwriting, totally incomprehensible after so long.

I say goodbye to my mother. It's like I'm going to a consultation—rather than a poetry reading—where I'll be told how long I have left to live.

"So, you show up in the *Messaggero* and don't say a fucking word."

Giovanni waves a newspaper in my face the moment he sees me; he's outside the office with Massimo and Luciano, along with Raffaella and some other women. I take the newspaper from Giovanni's hands. He points a big finger to the part I have to read. The list of cultural events in the city includes the reading that awaits me. My name appears among the poets.

"I found you, dear," says Adriana. Once again, I notice that undefined request in her eyes.

"Would you believe this guy?" Giovanni takes the newspaper back, scanning it for the few lines of the announcement. "The guest poets include . . . hang on, where are you . . . there . . . Daniele Mencarelli. I repeat, Daniele Mencarelli among the guest poets. Do you hear me?"

"It's no big deal. It only gets three lines." I try to end the conversation, but my words trigger a sudden change in Giovanni. Now irony seems to have turned to annoyance.

"What do you mean, no big deal? You're in a national newspaper. They're calling you a poet. That means nothing to you?"

"No, of course it's great, but when you do that sort of thing it's normal to end up in newspapers, reviews, articles."

"Hear that? It's normal to end up in newspapers when you do these important jobs. Not like us, right Dan? You're here by accident and you don't want to be a skivvy for life, isn't that right?"

"He's not the only colleague who's ended up in a newspaper. Remember Enzetto? He turned up in one too. He had four hundred ecstasy pills in his house. He was famous too."

Massimo's quip came right on cue, razor-sharp. Every colleague laughs, including Giovanni. I laugh too, but I can't forget everyone's pointed, cold stares.

"You lot want a cup of tea as well? A couple of pastries? Come on, or I'll be the one getting the blame. The four of you need to fix a problem in an operating theatre in the surgery department, sorting out a shutter they've contaminated. Go and give it a clean, then the company will come and sterilize everything."

I walk alongside Giovanni on the way to the department.

"Look, personally, I wouldn't even go to these readings."

Giovanni falls silent and so do I. After a few steps, he claps me on the shoulder with such force that I slam against a wall.

"Come on, poet, buy us a coffee before I pummel you."

A smile appears beneath his square goatee.

It's nice to feel accepted again. Massimo, a little further on, winks at me. He understood my predicament just as he now understands my joy. I don't need to tell him anything; my grateful glance is enough.

The surgical wards are like spaceships. Everything—at least on the surface—exists here protected, separated from the outside world. Before entering, we donned the obligatory space suit: the green worker scrubs, overshoes, cap and mask.

The contaminated room is the antechamber of an operating theatre. In order to change the belt of a roller shutter, some workers had to open the window, unaware of the damage they were causing: both the anteroom and operating theatre were declared unusable.

"Know how much this joke costs the hospital? The steriliza-tion company charges at least five million lire for an operating theatre."

Our job is limited to little more than dusting. The real work will be done by the company's specialists. We knuckle down.

"We've got to be careful here, Danny. There must be three billion lire worth of machinery in here. If we do any damage, we'll be working until we're three hundred."

The room is certainly impressive. Unfathomable machinery is scattered all around the central bed and a huge operating lamp hangs from the ceiling. I look through our stuff for gloves to wear. I always put on at least two pairs at a time, but the paper container is empty. I settle for a pair of surgical gloves. They're thicker and longer than the ordinary latex ones, almost coming up to my elbow. There's a small bar of soap in each pack for washing your hands; according to the instructions, it takes at least five minutes to properly clean them.

As I wipe the walls with disinfectant, my eyes roam the display cabinets at the sides of the room, filled with surgical tools. I de-duce this from the context, certainly not from my own knowledge of them. I wouldn't be surprised to see them in a machine shop, or—worse still—a torture chamber. Vises, hacksaws with gleam-ing teeth, retractors. The hardness of steel at the service of flesh.

After an hour or so, I can't ignore it anymore: industrial quantities of caffeine were the last straw for my bladder, already slackened by years of alcohol. I go to find the toilet.

Eight operating theatres open onto the corridor. Each door has a porthole for observing what's going on inside.

At the entrance to the operating ward, a nurse gave us clear instructions: work in the other operating rooms is proceeding as scheduled, and major operations are planned for that day, especially one in room four, which will go on for at least another eight hours. We have to act like ghosts, do our job, then disap-pear as soon as possible.

Room four is two doors beyond ours. I should go to the toilet, but that porthole is calling me. It's asking to be used, that's what it's there for.

The vault of an open chest, around six or seven green scrubs.

One glance is enough to realize my mistake, the latest in a very long series resulting from my pathological curiosity.

I'm totally stunned by that child, but perhaps what strikes me most are all those doctors accustomed to working on human gears, mechanics before a machine with a name and surname, with an engine that propels blood and fresh air into the lungs. What greatness a person can achieve, performing a miracle on Earth, adding years to a child's life. And how great pettiness can become, so great it turns into the iniquity of those who don't understand this mission's majesty and merely butcher for money.

At three-thirty, we finish cleaning in the operating ward. As the hours pass, the thought of the reading becomes ever more obsessive. Every now and then, I tell myself to drop out. Why should I subject myself to such nervous exertion? But that would mean losing the only space where my voice comes out authentically, with all the burden of love and inability to live that I bear every day.

"Dear."

As we're walking towards the office, Adriana joins me. She's not wearing a uniform; her shift is long over. When I realize she wants to talk to me, I signal to my three teammates to carry on ahead. Adriana is wearing a sweater similar to one of my mother's; she must be at least three sizes larger than her. I approach, but she remains silent, intimidated.

"Tell me, Adri."

It takes her enormous effort to speak.

"I've been wanting to ask you a favor for a while, ever since I heard you're a poet."

She falls silent again. I've seen that shame so many times. For an adult, talking about poetry—especially the first few times—is an act that requires great courage.

"You can talk to me freely, Adri."

"I've got a son, I think I told you. He's been unwell for three years. He's been to two specialists who each saw him for an hour and pumped him full of drugs, but in my view he just needs to open up to someone, to find someone who understands him. Then maybe he won't feel so lonely and he can start living normally again."

I certainly didn't expect this kind of request.

"What do the doctors say?"

"They both said it's bipolar disorder, but I don't think they really understood."

"Alright, bring him here any time."

Adriana seems reborn. She gives me a quick hug, then plants a kiss on my cheek. "Thanks dear. Is tomorrow afternoon O.K. for you? You start at five. Maybe we can meet here outside the bar around four."

"Perfect."

I don't know the purpose of this meeting, but I had no choice. Holed up in the tool room, taking turns to smoke so as not to reveal our presence, the entire team is resting, waiting for the stroke of eight. Luciano plays with his mobile phone. Massimo and Giovanni, sitting on some detergent boxes, chat about this and that. The conversation has turned to the hospital's director.

"Can you imagine? Fifteen million lire a month. That's one hundred and eighty a year, not to mention all the benefits he'll get, like his house and car."

"That said, it's not like he enjoys it. He's here morning to night. Anyway, how could he enjoy it? That guy is a church-goer."

"Church-goer, yeah right. He's a son of a bitch, that's for sure."

I listen without speaking, my attention turned inward to baleful thoughts connected to the reading. Somebody kicks me in the thigh.

"Hey, you alive?" It was Massimo.

"I'm alive, I'm alive. Let me remind you that your shoes—and I say yours because six months in I'm still using my own—have an iron toe cap, so you've got to kick gently." I give Massimo a kick. "Feel how soft that is? It's a kick from a trainer, a branded one too."

"Whatever, I get it. But what the hell happened to you? You're all white, silent. You look like you're dying."

"I'm not dying. It's just these readings I do are a burden. I'm shy. Besides, all that lot are full of themselves."

"What do you care? Actually, if they're full of themselves and you turn out to be better than them, you'll enjoy it twice as much."

Luciano, who until now had been staring at his mobile phone, suddenly approaches.

"Tell the truth. You fuck at these readings. You read, then maybe a girl comes over and compliments you, and there you go."

"I thought it was strange you weren't talking about pussy, Luci, but I have to disappoint you. In six years of readings, I've never picked up a girl, though maybe others manage."

"For fuck's sake, Dan. You don't feel like going. You're shitting yourself. You're not going to get laid. How about this? You go to my house and eat last night's leftovers. You spend the whole time sitting by yourself and I'll go instead of you. Agreed?" I look at Giovanni, at the fatherly face with which he asked this fake question.

"Gio, you won't believe this, but if I listened to my fear, I'd gladly switch places."

He's silent for a few seconds.

"Dan, can I tell you something?"

I immediately nod.

"You can fuck right off." And he punches me on the shoulder.

"You're right Gio, he should fuck off a little." Massimo associates words and deeds; a violent slap strikes the back of my head. Luciano, without saying anything, feels duty-bound to get involved. He delivers a blow on the shoulder that Giovanni already struck.

We clock out at eight sharp. In my reading outfit, complete with my bag, I say goodbye to the others, then set off alone. I stop for a few moments under Knock-Knock's window, but there's no sign of him.

"A glass of white."

The only positive aspect of this ordeal is the license I've granted myself.

I walk through the center of Rome, waiting for the moment the alcohol kicks in. I'm struck by this profound sense of loneliness. I should be enjoying my stroll, but I can't.

I'm in one of the most beautiful places in the world, surrounded by hundreds and hundreds of tourists who have come to marvel at this wonder, yet nothing captivates me. A sense of emptiness, an absence renewed at every step, every time a shop window displays my solitary image.

"A glass of white."

I've allowed myself exactly three drinks, the last of which I'll have just before I launch into the reading. Then it'll all be over, and I'll be able to breathe again.

There are already several people outside the gallery, including the group of guest poets. Some are friends, others less so, either through lack of acquaintance or mutual dislike.

The art gallery is a four-hundred-square-foot hole and it's packed. It's not like it takes a thousand people to fill it, but there must be at least seventy here. There are some Informalist paintings on the walls. Not particularly nice, at least in my opinion. Sad, if anything. There's an enormous wooden book at the end of this room, a sculpture by an attending artist; the poets will sit on that huge block to read. The whole situation makes my heart race downhill even faster than before. Before I show up, I take a twenty-yard detour, the distance required to reach a bar next door.

"A glass of white."

I've now reached the limit of my license, at least under the agreed terms.

Alcohol arrives with a wave of warmth and a sudden ability to indulge in hugs and bursts of affection. I squeeze into the little group of poets after warmly greeting everyone.

Before the reading starts, we discuss the usual things.

"Did you know? Mondadori is working on a new anthology. They say it'll be edited by Cucchi and Riccardi again."

"I didn't, but have you heard about Guanda? They want to stop the Fenice series. It would be a terrible loss."

Suddenly, a girl arrives from inside the gallery with a tray and glasses. The owner wants guests to try a wine made by her producer friend. The red flows crisp, full-bodied. A few minutes later, a guy covered in piercings makes the rounds with a sparkling white. Light, very light.

The poets are invited to sit on the wooden book in alphabetical order, so, a bit like at school, I'll be roughly in the middle.

Despite all the alcohol, I'm dreading that catafalque I'll have to get on to read. The poets stand on it somewhat constricted, half-sitting, in a seemingly uncomfortable position.

I don't know if I can do it. My body has lost its naturalness. I no longer feel natural in any situation, let alone on top of a mahogany book the size of a living room. The other poets, despite the discomfort of the seat, come and go just like that, so composed, calm. I'm not like them, I never will be, nor will I ever be the same as my teammates. I'm not like anyone.

"A glass of white."

"A glass of white."

"A glass of white."

When I return to the gallery, there are still a couple of poets to go, then it'll be my turn. They call my name. I smile at hearing it. I walk among the people sitting and watching me. An impenetrable blanket has now descended between me and those around me.

With my first glance at that big book, forgetfulness pounces. Everything goes dark. I've only some brief, blurred images of what comes next: a poet friend asking me to come and eat something with them, me declining with the excuse of tomorrow's work shift. Then more embraces, but I don't remember with whom or when.

I try my hardest to remember something from the reading. Nothing.

God knows how it went.

19

How did it go?"

"Brilliant. I read five new poems. They went down really well."

"That's not what I would've guessed from the state you were in when you got back."

"No, it went great. I actually felt relaxed."

My mother and I eat together. She's put a beautiful steak on my plate. She's a master at choosing meat. I haven't eaten for twenty-four hours, and I'm famished; she doesn't seem particularly hungry, just taking the occasional scoop from a tub of cream cheese.

"When I was putting you to bed last night, you were raving, as usual. You kept repeating that they'd opened a child's chest and they should close it again. You even cried."

"It's nothing. It's just that yesterday we did a job in an operating theatre. They were operating on a child next door."

That's all we say.

I leave home at half two. I have to be at the bar outside Bambino Gesù at four. Adriana and her son are waiting for me. Though I don't really know what we'll say to each other. I can't help myself, let alone someone else.

But my car is nowhere to be found. Immobile in the middle of the street, I attempt the unattemptable, to remember something, but I really don't know where to start. I check all the spots where—sober or drunk—I normally dump the car, but no luck, it's vanished.

It's three o'clock and the treasure hunt is at a standstill, leaving me helpless, swearing.

"If you're looking for your car, it's under the bridge on the road to Genzano."

I receive this information from the baker in the square, who—on more than a few nights—has had to interrupt his work to pick me up off the ground and take me home.

I find it with a ticket under the windscreen wiper. Here's what happens when you park with two wheels on a curb. I speed off without considering that the left side of the car is ten inches higher, on the curb. There's a resounding thud and I bounce inside the passenger compartment. Even cars are born with crosses to bear: some end up in the hands of respectable people; others finish up in mine. I caress it as it carries me to the hospital. The black dashboard—covered with encrusted dust—is where it likes to be petted.

Despite the Friday afternoon traffic, I manage to arrive on time. For parking, I have a deal with Littletooth, the illegal attendant I've named after the single tooth in his mouth. He knows my shifts and leaves a space for me. In return, I give him ten thousand a week, plus a few coffees. Walking briskly, I arrive at the bar on the Janiculum where we arranged to meet, but there's no sign of Adriana and her son. The lack of rain has turned the sky over Rome into suspended lead. Looking at it makes you almost want to stop breathing. Higher up—elevated to a very different air and sky—are the Castelli. Smog doesn't reach us. It doesn't dare.

"Dear."

Adriana comes up behind me. There's no one with her.

"He's sitting there. He's shy but he wants to talk. I'm going to the hospital so you can both feel more comfortable." She points to a boy on a bench.

"O.K.." I walk towards her son, then I'm stopped by a thought. "Adri, sorry, I don't know his name."

"Daniele, like you."

*

I sit on the bench, the only one in the row that isn't bathed in mid-afternoon sun. Daniele registers my arrival without looking at me. He's about my height with a protruding belly beneath a black T-shirt, long brown hair swept back in a ponytail, and an unkempt beard on his face, covering cheeks scarred by acne from former years. He turns towards me.

"Let me tell you right now, I'm here to make my mother happy, certainly not for my sake." Then he goes back to observing the nothingness on the opposite side to where I'm sitting.

"We've got the same name. What year were you born?"

Silence ensues. For a while, I comply, then it starts to pain me. Ever since I was a child, I've always regarded it as one of my faults, a void of words and sounds caused by my inability to be companionable, or by some misdeed that offended those around me.

"What year were you born?"

More silence.

"Look, your mother isn't expecting anything from this meeting. She only did it to get you to talk a little."

Daniele finally turns back to face me.

"I don't want to."

He said it slowly, articulating every sound. Now, as we regard each other a little longer, I can clearly see his eyes, the hatred in his pupils. He'd gladly kill me if he could. Suddenly I'm tremendously afraid. Daniele keeps his face pointed at mine.

"I don't know you and I don't want to know you. I was home, in my room, on my bed, then in she comes and tells me there's a very sensitive colleague who'd like to meet me. She dragged me out, but I was fine, fine. She doesn't want me to sit around and do nothing, looking at the ceiling, but I like looking at the ceiling, sitting still. Can I look at the ceiling? Can't I just look at it?" From silence to an avalanche of words at breakneck speed. A slight tremor makes his whole face dance. His forehead glistens with sweat. "Let's hear it then, what do you want to tell me that's so important? Are you a sage? A visionary? Do you speak to God? To the Devil? Or do you work for the services? Do you know the names of the saints?"

His mouth hangs open. White drool dribbles down each side.

"I asked if you know the names of the saints. Well, do you?"

"You mean of all the saints?"

"Yes, every single one. From first to last."

"No, I don't know them."

"Then how do you think you can help someone like me? I know all of them, all of them. Want to hear them?"

"No, I believe you."

"Listen. Achilleo Adalberto Agata Agnese Agostino Alberto Alfonso Ambrogio Andrea Angela."

"Oh God, it's four-thirty. Sorry, I have to start work."

I leave him on the bench. I only glance back once. He keeps looking in my direction, his mouth open, or so it seems. He's still spewing out the names of the saints.

"So, how did it go?" Adriana's voice makes me jump. She was waiting behind the hospital gate. "I was hoping you'd talk to him longer. He's a little aggressive at first, but he gradually calms down."

There's hope in her eyes that I really don't know how to nurture.

"I'm not a doctor, Adri, so take what I'm saying with a pinch of salt, but I think Daniele needs what the doctors told you."

Adriana doesn't even let me finish. Hope instantly died on her face. She walks off towards her son.

"Adri, don't see doctors and psychiatric drugs as a bad thing. I took them when I was twenty and they helped me. Let them treat him. You'll find things improve."

She stops abruptly, looking at me in a new way.

"I thought you were a sensitive guy who could understand other sensitive people, but clearly I was wrong."

"Adri, sensitivity is a dangerous subject. Your son has vulnerabilities, problems. If you don't acknowledge this, you'll never help him."

"You must be the one with problems, not him."

Adriana walks away. I watch her cross the street, come up to her son, and gently touch his shoulder.

I head towards our office. I can feel a wound somewhere, a fresh gash, but I've no ammunition against myself. I simply said what anyone would. I tried to voice the truth, nothing more.

The twentieth century will come to an end in a few months and with it a whole millennium. If I could be granted one wish, I'd ask for a total ban—from the year 2000 onwards—on the concept of "sensitivity," at least when used to fantasize about the human spirit. A single concept for thousands upon thousands of inaccuracies, dangerous do-goodisms, and delayed or never completed realizations.

"What happened to you? Looks like you got beaten up."

Massimo is sitting outside the office. Giovanni and Luciano haven't arrived yet.

"What are you on about? Adriana wanted me to see her son. He's sick. I mean, really sick. She got mad when I told her, but what could I do?"

"Well, what could you do? Nothing, if he's sick. Unfortunately, mothers are always the last to understand certain things about their children. It's normal, actually."

"You're right. Tell that to mine."

Massimo strokes his moustache, observing me.

"How do you mean?"

"Nothing. Let's just say I've caused her a fair amount of trouble . . ."

"Ah, whatever, who hasn't been through a stint of fucking up? Everyone."

I wish I could tell Massimo that my own stint has carried on undisturbed for years.

"Look how cute they are. They're like Chip and Dale." Giovanni's voice reaches us from behind. Luciano stands beside him.

"You and that skinny rake are cute too. You look like Abbott and Costello." Massimo has one of the quickest tongues I've ever known.

"Come on, let's go and clean up that fucking collection center."

Split into pairs, we walk down to the changing room. The milky sky is getting heavier.

"We're going to drop dead today," comments Giovanni, sweeping back his sweaty hair.

"Luckily, there's a brand-new air-conditioning system in the collection center." As Luciano replies, he takes a tissue and wipes his glasses, the ones I paid for to replace the broken pair.

At the end of the descent, we pass a security guard. He's opening—with one of the many keys in his bunch—the green door to the little house for dead children.

"That guy is from Ciociaria. A nurse from his village told me he's stinking rich. He owns a load of land." Giovanni is referring to the guard.

"Lucky him." Massimo and I respond together, perfectly synchronized.

Amir is in the changing room. He greets us with a nod.

"Hey there, pizza man," says Massimo.

"Talking of which, when are you lot coming to have pizza at my place? I'll send you all to heaven."

Giovanni looks at each of us in turn. "Not a bad plan. How about we go out for a pizza together tomorrow night?"

Everyone immediately likes the idea.

"Then we'll arrange a time after the blood collection center. Nice one, Amir."

On the way to our tool room, we continue discussing arrangements for the next evening.

"Maybe later we can go to some clubs. Some strip clubs. Something like that."

Giovanni pauses, weighing up Luciano's words. "When's your birthday, Luci?"

"End of November. Why?"

"Your very own Giovanni is going to give you a present. I'll rent you a whore. I'll hand you a hundred thousand lire and you can go to some brothel and get a fifteen-stone slut so she'll run you ragged. Then you'll keep quiet for a few months at least."

Luciano takes offence, while we laugh shamelessly.

Several people are standing outside the dead children's house.

They're not Italian. They have olive skin, black hair. Maybe Mexican, Peruvian.

I take a long look at one of them.

A thought, a strange slowing of my heart.

I freeze.

"Dan?" It's Massimo calling me.

"You guys go ahead. I'll be right there."

I take a few steps, just enough for my eyes to focus on those faces, their features, the words in Spanish.

And inside, that growing thought.

I take more steps, then even more.

I haven't been this close to the green door since my first day at work.

From inside the little house, voices overlap, some crying uncontrollably, others clinging to prayers.

A step. Another step.

Now I'm just a few feet from the entrance. Maybe if I

stretched my neck I'd already be able to see, but I don't have the strength.

Another step. One more to go. The last.

It's him.

It's really him.

It's Knock-Knock.

He's wearing a formal suit, a tie, his hair carefully combed.

It's Knock-Knock.

Why is Knock-Knock dead?

His folded hands clasping a rosary, his frozen face, all gone. Why?

I try to remove everything from my eyes. I want to tear them out.

I feel a hand rest on my shoulder. I turn around. It's the evil nurse, the one who kicked me out of Knock-Knock's room. Her eyes are filled with tears.

"He didn't make it."

I stare at her. "I don't know anything."

She brings her face close to my ear.

"Alfredo suffered from recurrent infections. Two years ago, they gave him a double kidney transplant, but he never recovered from the operation. His kidneys failed tonight. There was nothing we could do."

Alfredo.

Knock-Knock was Alfredo. My cuckold, my wordless companion, was called Alfredo.

"He'd just come back. I saw he'd lost weight, but I didn't expect this."

"Back from where?"

"He and I used to play through the window, but I hadn't seen him for a long time."

"Alfredo hadn't left the hospital for at least a year. He was going back and forth to the intensive care unit. That's why there were times when you didn't see him."

He was always here, commanded by the disease, and I didn't understand a thing.

This time, crying is no use. An irrepressible rage mounts at full speed, a fury that ignites muscle after muscle, nerve after nerve.

Indolence. The spiritual poverty of those who don't want to truly sink into other peoples' lives and pain. These are just the first things of which I accuse myself.

I can do nothing but hate myself for the friendship I could've given him, for what he—in vain—perhaps expected from me.

My feet and legs can no longer hold still. I try everything to stop myself moving, but I can't. I have to go out. To get moving.

I look at Knock-Knock—Alfredo—one last time. I'd like to go and caress him, but I can't.

May this place burn to a cinder, and the Earth with it.

The only cure is to forget everything.

My teammates are preparing the equipment for the once-over. I approach them upset, but I don't care about anything now.

"Guys, I've got a problem. I don't feel well. Tell Fabio I've left."

They want to stop me, to understand, but I don't give them time to do anything. I don't even get changed. I leave the hospital in uniform. After all, there's no need to be well-dressed for what I have to do.

"A bottle of white."

At the first bar I come across.

I get back in the car. My hands are sweaty and I have to use my teeth to remove the aluminum cap. Just one long sip—I'd set out to finish the whole bottle in a single gulp—and I've won.

I find myself in the Viale Marconi area. I've got two hundred thousand lire in my pocket. I can finish the job no problem.

"A bottle of white."

I'd like to empty the second bottle like the first, but I have to retire midway through the race. I couldn't do it. It takes me two more swigs to polish it off.

Alcohol enters my bloodstream, but there's no softness, no pleasure. Just a fire kindled under the already incandescent rage.

"A bottle of white."

I drink a quarter of it, then place it on the seat next to mine. I'll finish this a little at a time. I've now arrived in an area I don't know, maybe Magliana, maybe somewhere behind Garbatella.

Coughing turns into retching. I manage to open the door. I vomit as the car rolls along. It knows how to drive itself by now.

One of those new churches. The irregular design is intended to tone down the grey of the concrete. Sad architecture with no history, born old.

I head for the first few benches and sit down.

Three ladies are repeating the rosary. Their voices blend until they become one. I don't know the prayer they're chanting. I know so few. The rest is deserted. It's just me and them.

Even the crucifix is modern. It's an impressive work. The cross is made of light-colored wood, perhaps ash, while Christ seems to be crafted from white ceramic. Unlike the rest of it, he retains his solemnity. I stand there, motionless, gazing at Christ's body on the cross. I wish he'd talk to me. I'd only have to hear his voice once and all would become peaceful, clear. Even the blackness where Knock-Knock now dwells would be less frightening. But Christ can't speak. If he ever did, it was with people with spring water in place of a heart, certainly not people like me.

I don't know how much time passes before I stand up again. The three women keep counting their rosaries with the occasional glance in my direction. Before leaving, I pause at a candle rack and pull a five-hundred-lira coin from my pocket to put in the offertory box, but the slot is too narrow and my balance is completely drunk. The slot tries to elude me. Every attempt finishes off to the side. I leave the coin nearby. I light a candle with the flame of a nearly extinguished one. Knock-Knock burns in the center of the flame. I can see him perfectly, but I can't touch him. Then I leave.

Night falls. The bottle sits empty beside me.

I fail to brake in time at a traffic light, hitting the car in front.

A girl gets out, furious. I get out in turn, but as soon as my feet touch the ground, I tumble over.

"Look at you, you should be ashamed!" she shouts. I pick myself up and charge towards her. She pushes me. I do the same, hurling her against her car.

"Oi, asshole, you're attacking a woman!" Three guys approach from a nearby bar. I'm not afraid of them. I face them with a smile on my lips.

"And what the fuck do you care?"

Out of nowhere comes a very hard punch to my temple. By the time I've realized and thrown a couple myself, I'm kicked in the back and fall flat on the ground. I try to defend myself to no avail, then more kicks. I shield my skull with my hands, but the rest of my body is no man's land.

20

I recognize the hospital.

As well as the two people at the entrance to the room, talking to a doctor in hushed voices.

My mother and father.

"How did I get here?"

My father is sitting on a chair next to the bed, while my mother is still beside the doctor.

"You're asking us?"

I struggle to keep my eyes open. I feel pain above one eye, in my back.

"Don't you remember anything?" my father asks me.

"Blackness. I remember a girl I rear-ended, then three guys grabbing me, pounding me. That's all. Where did you find me?"

"You got home and passed out as soon as you came in. You were covered in dirt. With a swollen eye. We carried you."

"What did they do to me? Have I broken something?"

"The doctor said it's probably nothing serious. They need to take an X-ray of your back. They already did your head, but he wants to keep you in hospital. Not because of the beating."

"Because of the usual, then."

My father nods, overcome with irrepressible despair. It's almost like he feels guilty about crying, or perhaps he's just ashamed.

"Yes, same as ever. Alcohol and psychological disorders."

"Tell them this time I won't stay even if they tie me up. I'll get the X-rays and come home."

My father gets up, standing an inch from my face.

"I don't know if you've still got a home, Dan. I can't keep on living unless you go. At least we won't see you dying bit by bit."

"Fair enough."

I leave the hospital at three on Saturday afternoon.

The X-ray of my back didn't show any injuries. Just one hip hurts, but that's normal.

The X-ray of my head was also negative. The casing, anyway.

The doctor wanted to admit me. He told me so several times. He even threatened me with compulsory hospitalization. When I explained what had happened to me, about Knock-Knock, he eventually let me go.

I find my brother and sister at home. They stop talking as soon as I enter.

"Hi."

They don't return the greeting. I can't really blame them.

I go straight to my room, undressing in slow motion due to my sore hip. My eye doesn't hurt at all. It's swollen. Maybe it'll turn black. But otherwise, it's no big deal.

The Toradol is still coursing through my body. As soon as I lay down on my bed, I feel sleep will come easily.

I sink into Knock-Knock's image. His face fills the black cavity of my mind. "Forgive me," I ask him with the voice in my head. "Forgive me" for not having been there, for never having heard the melody of your voice, which I can never listen to again.

For Sunday lunch—I immediately recognize it—my mother has made beef shank with tomato sauce. But my nose is drawn to another smell, overpowered by the meat, but present, delicate. I have to see it to solve the enigma: runner beans, also with sauce. The table is set for nine. My brother and sister will join us for lunch. I'm not hungry, and I don't think my presence is advisable. It usually takes a while to mollify my family, although for each of them the timing varies. My sister is the most malleable, the one who takes the least time to go from crying to smiling. My brother, by contrast, is the slowest, perhaps because his head—born mature—is the furthest removed from mine. My mother and father are in the middle, but they no longer rank.

"Go and take a shower. Your brother and sister are coming for lunch. You have to be there too."

That "you have to be there" is more than a hint. The subject of the lunch will obviously be me. I'll be confronted with the usual list of pretexts I've supposedly come up with to hurt myself, followed by "What's wrong with you?" "Why don't you love yourself?" and so on.

Standing in the shower, I take a look at the bruise on my hip. The vaguely circular shape must be from the toe of the shoe that struck me, or perhaps it's just my imagination. My eye is swollen, turning dark between my eyelid and eyebrow. It only hurts if I quickly rotate my pupil. It's bearable, all things considered.

When I go down to the kitchen, my siblings have already arrived. We don't even say hello. I throw myself at my nephews, who greet me joyfully as always. We lie on the sofa in a frenzy of hugs and kisses. The eldest has recently started to say a few words. He mangles my name as he plays.

Who knows where Knock-Knock is now. Perhaps en route to his home country or bound for some local cemetery. Maybe he and his family were living in Italy. Who knows.

We take our usual positions around the table, but there's something abnormal about this lunch. I can tell from the fact that no one has touched a thing on their plate. Usually, as soon as we sit down, we—each to a varying extent—start picking at the various courses. But today everyone is motionless. Almost like eating isn't the reason we've gathered.

"Dan, we've got something to tell you."

My brother has been chosen to communicate with me.

"There's a rehabilitation community outside Viterbo for people with alcohol abuse problems. It's not free, but if we each chip in, we can manage."

On a few other occasions, they've speculated about something like this. Care homes, specialized hospitals. But in the past it was a hypothesis suggested by doctors, nothing concrete.

"You're all crazy."

"Why exactly are we crazy?"

My brother snapped back at me, but now I can't do the same to him. What is it that makes them crazy? There's nothing unreasonable about what they're proposing, but it's the last thing I want to do. Right now, moving me away from home would mean killing me. They don't know it, but this house, my town, and they themselves are the only things keeping me alive, protecting me. But this is sentimental talk and—after years of disasters—the time for words has passed. I've given them too many, of every kind in existence.

"What am I supposed to do about work?"

This is the only thing that's come to mind, though after Knock-Knock I thought I'd never set foot there again. My brother is dancing about in his chair. He's struggling to keep his cool. I know him.

"Since when have you had scruples about anything? You suddenly care so much about work and we're really supposed to believe that?"

"I can't leave my work. Only the four of us can do some of the cleaning jobs. I'd be leaving them in the shit."

"But you don't give a fuck about all the shit you've thrown at us for the last four years, do you?"

My brother is on the verge of exploding. No possible answer would defuse him, nor can I think of anything convincing.

"I'm going upstairs. My hip really hurts."

I slowly make my way up the staircase to the bedrooms.

My whole family stares down at their plates. Only my nephews smile at me, simply because they don't have a sense of judgement yet, otherwise they wouldn't look at me either.

"You two have got to make him! If you don't acknowledge this, he'll kill you both. Do you understand?"

My brother's voice accompanies me to my room. I can still hear it when I close the door.

It's just after one and there's no way I'll get back to sleep. If I could follow my instincts, I'd go out drinking, but it would be over the dead bodies of my whole family. I hear someone approaching the door, one step at a time. It's my brother. His face doesn't bode well. I instinctively get out of bed. He won't stop staring at me.

"I came up intending to kick your ass. Properly, like I've never done before. Once and for all. You've been destroying us for years, sending us to bed dreading the sound of the telephone. The woman downstairs is your mother as well as mine. Dad too." My brother takes a step towards me, and I take a step back. "Actually, that's the only reason I came up. I really wanted to lock us in so no one would bother us. But then." He grabs the desk chair with one hand, pulling it towards him, and sits down. "Then I got obsessed with trying to remember the last time I hit you. At first, I couldn't remember. In the hallway of the old house, over a ball game. Remember?"

It takes no effort.

"I remember, yeah. If mum hadn't separated us, we would've killed each other."

We both fixate on the memory. He starts to cry, doing his best not to let it show. When my brother cries, he has an uncanny resemblance to my father. He gets up and leaves without another glance in my direction.

A myriad of elements leads me to an absolute, unquestionable certainty. This exact moment—right now—is the unhappiest of my life. The amount of purposely sought misfortunes adds up to all that I've passively witnessed. Knock-Knock. Stefano. The whole army of children devoured by various diseases. I'm at the lowest point. At the center of the Earth. I come to this certainty on the very day of the week I most detest, Sunday. In the afternoon, to cap it all. Perfection never achieved.

21

It's a hot, sunny Monday. Rome is burning at thirty-three degrees in the shade. To think that yesterday was the last day of summer.

At six in the morning, the air is already sultry, though the sun hasn't appeared yet.

When they see me, my teammates lower their gaze. Only Massimo continues staring me in the eye. Then he follows suit.

"Morning."

No one greets me back.

Giovanni gets up to go to the changing room, passing me without a word. Massimo and Luciano follow him. I do the same.

There's the little dead children's house, once home to Knock-Knock and all his brothers and sisters who ended up in this hospital. A sudden wave of nausea. By the time I realize, it's already passed.

"What do I have to do? Get down on my knees? Beg your forgiveness one by one?"

I can no longer stand my teammates' silence. You could hear a pin drop in the changing room. Never has the atmosphere been so heavy. As usual, I'm the cause of it all.

"No, honestly, tell me. What do I have to do? I had a problem and needed to run off. It's not like you want to treat me this way forever."

Giovanni, in his underwear, comes right up to me.

"We don't want anything, Dan, but you can't expect to

behave the way you did and then for us to be all chummy without even getting pissed off. One moment you showed up with two eyes full of tears, upset. The next you run off without even telling us what happened to you, for fuck's sake."

I don't know how to react, whether to tell him and the others the truth.

"Gio, on Friday I got a phone call from a girl. There, now you know. My world fell apart."

Giovanni continues to stare at me for a while, then nods and goes back to his locker to finish getting dressed. Luciano and Massimo are ready.

"To make up for it, all the coffees are on me today, happy?"

"Just today? You mean all week."

Before going to the office, we stop by the café. A doctor—a gentleman in his fifties—is celebrating his birthday. He's paying for his colleagues' breakfast at the till. When he turns around, it's my turn.

"Is it your birthday too?" he asks with a smile.

"No, I've got to pay for the round to make amends."

"What did you do?"

"If only you knew."

As we head towards the office, I notice Massimo deliberately slowing down. He starts walking beside me.

"I for one don't believe that crap about a phone call from a girl. Something happened to you in here."

We've now arrived right under the windows where—over the course of these months—I played with Knock-Knock.

"See those windows?"

"Sure, I see them."

"From the first day I set foot in here, I played with a child who used to look out from there. First from one, then from another. This carried on for months. I only went up once to try and actually meet him. On Friday, I found him in the mortuary. Now do you understand?"

Massimo remains silent, his face pained as we start walking again.

"You're the only one who knows, Max."

"Why should you be ashamed to feel sorrow? What do you care if they all know?"

"Yeah, well, I'd rather they don't."

Massimo stops, looking me straight in the eye. He grips my shoulders.

"Dan, you worry too much, way too much. People who don't feel sorrow for others should be the ones worrying, not you."

Giovanni and Luciano are waiting for us outside the office, along with Fabio.

"Window day today. We've got to do the whole of the Salviati."

"Nice. At least we'll get tanned."

It's seriously difficult to clean windows in the blazing sun; it takes great skill to avoid leaving smears. Now I've mastered the wiper, every pane comes back to life under my hands. It just takes me one circular motion and job done. We've decided to start on the top floor, the fifth, split into pairs as usual.

The problem isn't so much cleaning the glass, as balancing on a ledge without any kind of protective harness, and I have all sorts of balance issues. The windows in the Salviati are also very large. We start with the inner side, a piece of cake, followed by the outer side, the dangerous one. To clean it, you have to climb a ladder facing the wide-open window. You could close the large wooden shutters, but that would make it impossible to see the work you're doing. I'm also handicapped by my shoes, which aren't non-slip like the others', so I have to be extremely careful, especially as the hours pass and soapy water from the wiper ends up on the ladder's iron steps. My feet often slip, but luckily I always manage to catch myself. Massimo, who doesn't suffer from vertigo, whistles as he works. He's attempted to start some sort of conversation a few times, but I can't bring myself to speak, let alone look in his direction. I get severe vertigo when I watch him in action. Fortunately, the fifth floor is soon complete.

We've just started the fourth, when Giovanni's mobile rings. It's Fabio: a child has thrown up in a clinic in the Spellman and he has no one to send. Giovanni looks at Massimo. It's usually the least senior in the team who has to handle these chores, just as I did on my first day of work, but I raise my hand like I'm at school.

"No worries, Gio. I'll go."

I'd rather a floor covered in vomit than a window sixty feet high.

Before going to the Spellman, I have to stop by the tool room to fetch a trolley with buckets and brooms. I cut through Sant'Onofrio since it's the shortest route and in this hot weather it's better to walk indoors than along the scorching avenues.

A young couple are standing near the Art Nouveau window. The mother holds a boy in her arms, while the father plays with him. He shows him the fountain in the internal garden, and makes him laugh, pulling faces and sticking his tongue out. When I'm no more than a yard away from them, the two parents turn around, along with their child. My step falters, my breathing too. The little boy must be three years old. Apart from his eyes, he doesn't have a face. In place of a nose and mouth, there are holes of red flesh. Keeping my eyes trained on the marble floor, I slip past them without a glance back. In the tool room, as I prepare the trolley, I come to the conclusion that I've reached saturation point. Enough. With this hospital, with all the sick, crippled, shapeless, dead children. Enough. I smoke a cigarette, then another. I waste time hoping the young couple and their disfigured son have left.

The child's laughter comes first. They're still there. But they're no longer alone. An elderly nun stands before them, bending over, her face grazing the boy's dreadful visage.

"You're mummy and daddy's handsome boy, aren't you?"

She takes a little hand and kisses it. Perhaps ticklish, he bursts out laughing. The nun must be over eighty. Her face is plump, white as milk.

"So, you're not just handsome, you're nice too. Do you like that?"

To his delight, she runs her little hand over his mouth, his chin. Then the nun straightens up, looking at the mother and father.

"Hear that laugh of his? This boy doesn't have silver inside. He has gold, living gold."

She kisses him, oblivious to his face, to everything.

I continue pushing the trolley with buckets and brooms.

I'm stunned. I can't understand or decipher.

I've witnessed something simultaneously human and alien, like a ritual from a faraway land. I can't find the inner tools to translate it into my own language.

The morning draws to an end in this state of sober intoxication. I've tried every possible approach. I've attempted to brush off what I saw as the delirium of an old woman dressed in grey. Then as the fanaticism of a nun deaf and blind to pain, who wanted to attest to the supremacy of her God in every way, even faced with that disfigurement. Then as the performance of a talented actress who—maybe a second later, in the privacy of a toilet—washed her mouth after kissing that shapeless face. But no interpretation can bridge the gap between what I saw and logic.

From time to time, Massimo tried to rouse me from my torpor. On a couple of occasions, he even succeeded for a few minutes, but then I relapsed, sinking into that scene, into the two faces pressed together, her words, his laughter.

The Janiculum Hill—normally invaded by tourists from all over—has no shady corner available today. Many Romans, especially elderly people, have also come up here to seek a modicum of cool air under the maritime pines, the large, lush palm trees.

It's one o'clock. I walk to my car in shorts and sandals, then change my mind. I head for the Lungotevere, a vein marred by a row of cars. When I get there, instead of taking the bridge that would lead me towards the center, I descend the stairs to the riverside.

Apart from a few runners and a couple of cyclists, it's just me and the Tiber. I walk with my eyes on the bank. The murky green water, the objects slowly dragged along by the current, mostly rubbish from God knows where. From here, the noise of the city arrives muffled, helpless. My eyes slowly familiarize themselves with the environment. River animals—invisible just a second before—start to materialize one by one: groups of ducks, motionless seagulls floating by, huge nutrias half-submerged in the water, silvery as they dart along.

The heat is really suffocating, along with the smell of the river. It took me months to recognize it. You mostly notice it at night, or in the morning at dawn, before the car fumes take over.

I don't know why I'm here, what I'm looking for. I just know one thing for sure: what I've seen speaks to me like something new. I didn't think there were any first experiences left to live.

22

It's a slow fire, silently smoldering ever since it entered my eyes.

The last two nights were spent doing routine cleaning. Giovanni occasionally rebuked me, not so much because I wasn't doing my job, but because I barely responded to his jokes. Massimo also tried to snap me out of this state several times, but also eventually threw in the towel.

"Forget it, Gio, he's a poet. He's got his own shit."

My three teammates are behaving well despite all my quirks. They're leaving me alone because they understand I need to be by myself. Perhaps for the first time since my birth, I'm experiencing silence without feeling guilty about it.

Even at home, a kind of rarefied truce prevails.

My parents have made no further attempt to talk to me about rehab, or about anything else for that matter. When we pass each other around the house, we just exchange glances, little else.

There was a rainstorm last night. The Lazio coast was battered by wind and water. It also rained in Rome, as well as in the Castelli. Summer has disappeared with the arrival of the rain. We'll discuss it again next year. Now it's sunny again, though not excessively so. There's a light, cool wind blowing, a reminder of the bad weather.

I tried for at least two hours, then gave up. I went to bed this morning. Usually after the second night I can sleep quite easily, but not today. Finally, around eight, I got up. I can't endure a night without sleep. My psyche can't handle it. I need to interrupt the flow of life, to disconnect from myself. When I skip sleep completely, I succumb to nerves even more than usual.

On my way to Rome, I'm hoping for an afternoon without any particular hassle or too much work. My body wouldn't be able to cope. Starting with my head.

Even when I don't think about it, I'm there, in the corridor of the Sant'Onofrio pavilion, confronted with the same scene endlessly sent and replayed by my mind. I try to detach myself from it in vain: after all, whatever its meaning, why not leave it among the events that have already taken place, one of the many memories scattered through anyone's past? But I can't. Simply because this option isn't available to me.

Since Monday, I've made a habit of going down from the Janiculum Hill to the Lungotevere, and down again to the riverside. I stay there watching the current. For me, accustomed to the stillness of Lake Albano, it's really extraordinary. I've found my own little spot, a marble step less dirty and malodorous than the others, right next to the water. I sit with my feet dangling, looking at everything and nothing.

It's eleven-twenty. My shift starts at one, still an eternity away. The river doesn't seem to have noticed the overnight rain. It doesn't look swollen, nor more enraged. It flows with the same lethargy as ever.

And again, the need to understand, to comprehend. I'd like to be able to explain the how and why of what I've seen, to be able to possess it among known things. Only then will I be able to overcome this paralysis.

On the moving water—murky at the top, dark as the sunless sky that's now towering above everything—I see myself reflected, carried away, yet always present to myself. The water flows, drags, but I'm still here.

Like all beloved things, transformed by the time that bears

us, but untouched within. Immutable beneath the crust of the current.

Like that boy's face, handsome beyond the rind that runs across it.

We don't need to understand, to comprehend.

We need to embrace all that's human with every bit of strength we're granted.

To arrive at beauty that knows no decay, the first and inviolable nucleus.

To face horror in order to break through it.

Here's the supremacy of the love I saw in that nun's eyes. A summit, a height destined for few. Only for those who never retreat when faced with reality, never closing their eyes. With boundless courage in their blood, stronger than any fear, any selfishness.

You can't get there without courage.

The past few years of my life suddenly flash before my eyes. So many words, names of drugs and illnesses, only to say that I lack the courage to live and see the people I love live, accepting the axe of fate. Because that's the only way it can be, consuming myself in proximity, in accepting every possible horror by experiencing it for what it really is: a diaphragm. A black veil to tear off. Behind that veil, we resist like children, all of us. Always.

I'll lose the light of this moment, whether a little at a time or all at once, I don't know.

But I'll bear witness to it forever because just one of these moments is enough to illuminate a whole life.

I arrive at Bambino Gesù slightly out of breath: going downhill is easy; coming back uphill from the Lungotevere a lot less so.

At the entrance barrier, after weighing every word, even the pauses between them, I pick up my mobile.

"Mum, I'm quitting today. No more."

My mother is silent. Only her breathing reaches me, then I hear her stop what she was doing.

"Now what gives you so much conviction?"

"It's not about conviction or realizing something. I can't let myself run away anymore or have clouded vision. I want to face up to things."

Silence returns. She resumes what she was doing, perhaps cleaning the floor.

"I gave birth to you, but your rebirth is entirely up to you."

23

At three in the morning, the world seems dead.

Everyone except me.

It's my first weekend without alcohol, my first Saturday night.

Yesterday, at midnight, we finished the once-over of the blood collection center. That precise moment effectively marked the start of my alcohol-free life.

I rushed home, then to bed.

Due to weariness, the many days disturbed by the vision of my nun, I fell asleep almost immediately.

Daytime on Saturday was one void after another.

The lack of wine didn't manifest itself violently, but with sighs, half-words spoken in my ear. I felt nostalgia, but the possession of my freedom was stronger than any other feeling. A monstrosity to fill, not knowing with what. With whom. In the end, it all turned into a very slow waste of time, a straggling loneliness, barely illuminated by a film on television, one smoked cigarette after another.

I tried to go out, but I didn't understand the point, the necessity. Going to shops doesn't interest me, let alone more complex activities such as visiting a museum or exhibition. It's better not to give a convalescent overly strong emotions.

My parents observe me from a distance, occasionally asking how I'm doing. You can see their fear. They're afraid any gesture will break the spell. This time, they really believe it; their greatest fear is the reverse of the hope they're cherishing.

My brother and sister also came by. They too spoke with their eyes.

Here I am. Three-fifteen. Saturday night.

On television it's all informercials, pay-per-minute sex lines, and unwatchable series. The music of recent years is also off limits to me; it's like putting on the soundtrack of an action film without any action. Besides, there are too many false memories; the real ones have been digested by forgetfulness.

From time to time, visions appear in my mind, scenes of wonderful boozing. It's evil's invitation to retrace my steps, to pick up where I left off.

It's not its attacks that frighten me. It's something deeper and more tangible that fills my bed with concern.

It's this transitional period between what I've been in the past few years and what I'm going to be. It's the construction of the new me that really terrifies me.

An individual with interests, relationships, a life filled with normality.

All things I can no longer even pronounce.

Around me, I have nothing, no one.

I've dug a trench and filled it with white wine.

I have my family, Davide, and a few other poet friends. Nothing else.

The serious part isn't the absences, but the total inability to fill them.

I didn't used to be like that. I knew how to act around people, how to have fun.

But I have the hospital, my job.

After all, in there I've returned to being able to live without alcohol.

I laugh and make others laugh.

I talk and listen.

I actually have everything.

Everything that has taken my life and turned it upside down is inside the hospital.

One gram at a time, limb by limb, right up to my heart, my brain.

When I think of all the encounters, the experiences, the aberration, and the enchantment within every single moment. And the multitude of words travelling through my mind.

I was already reborn.

The first day I set foot in Bambino Gesù.

24

Today is my sister's birthday. The first of October.

With a cigarette in the corner of my mouth, I'm finishing the process of de-waxing the linoleum in the hematology day hospital using the scrubber-dryer. Massimo has started waxing the doctors' rooms, where Giovanni and Luciano are finishing the high dusting.

It's the dead of night. Two-twenty on Wednesday.

I haven't drunk for over ten days. There are moments of discouragement, but I cope with them like an illness that has to be endured.

You need to wait it out, knowing full well that relapses are lurking, usually worse than the disease itself. The urge to drink—the real one, as violent as a slap—has crept up a few times. I've chased it away with cigarettes—I'm down to two and a half packs of MS—and by taking refuge among people. At home, with my father and mother. At work, with my three teammates.

Now I'm a virtuoso with the scrubber-dryer, perhaps—no, definitely—with a good deal of recklessness. I think of cowboys in rodeos, when they raise their hand to the crowd astride a skittish thoroughbred trying its best to unseat them.

A corner of the large waiting room is particularly dirty. The linoleum is stained with something dark that even the abrasive disc on the scrubber-dryer can't remove. As I push with all my strength, my eyes turn to the wall before me.

It's completely covered with photographs: all the children

who have passed through this day hospital. I quickly scan through them. Children—with illnesses of varying severity—of every age and race, many from Africa, as well as Slavs. There are also some Knock-Knocks with the same gleaming teeth and jet-black hair.

That's how the idea comes to me, nearly knocking the scrubber-dryer out of my hands.

As we finish the once-over, I get lost in the details, every single one. The whole thing doesn't just seem beautiful, but necessary.

Massimo made occasional attempts to talk to me. I could see his mouth moving, but couldn't tune into his voice.

"Guys, he's away with the fairies again," he finally pronounced.

Observing my trancelike state, my teammates joked about it, and I—in the few moments I was present—did the same.

We punch our timecards at five. Only four workers are clocking out, but at least twenty are ready to start their shifts. Adriana is among them. I've made every effort to talk to her. I searched for her, but she wouldn't listen to me anymore. It hurts me to meet her eyes, but I've no reason to reproach my-self. Adriana just so happens to have now joined the entourage of Marianna, the union rep. I'll never know for sure, but I can't help thinking that this new bond is something to do with me.

With Marianna, it's no longer the time for wisecracks, glances aimed—with feigned nonchalance—at my and other people's shoes. Now complete indifference reigns, antipathy declared without fear. I've been working at the hospital for seven months. Every time the cooperative has sent safety shoes in my size, she's pounced on them like they were solid gold. I've complained to Fabio and Antonio, but neither the foremen, nor anyone else at the cooperative has any interest in standing up to a union member over a pair of shoes.

Giovanni, Massimo, Luciano, and I agree to meet at one

o'clock. In less than eight hours, we'll start the Thursday after-noon shift.

As I walk towards the car, my eyes command me to stop and turn back.

It's daybreak. The sun looms just behind Monte Cavo and the Castelli Romani. It looks like the world's first dawn. After all that muggy weather, the view clouded by heat and smog, everything this morning appears with the intensity of its true colors. Leaning against the balustrade of the viewing area, I pause to watch. Every single particle of the cosmos seems to be in harmony with its surroundings. Nothing jars. There's no unhappiness as far as the eye can see. This is how God reveals himself. He speaks in these instants, the moment your breath stops.

The idea I had in the hematology day hospital is still there, resting on my shoulder. It clung to me throughout the jour-ney home and then in the shower, talking to me, constantly de-manding my attention. I'm overcome with a sense of impotence because I really don't know how to transform it from a simple idea into reality. What should I do? Who should I ask for help?

I get into bed, attempting to sleep with all the willpower I can muster, but I can feel it beside me. An idea needs no sleep. It knows no tiredness.

At twelve-thirty, with barely a couple of hours' rest, I arrive at the hospital. With my head down, hands in my pockets, I walk towards the changing room. As I pass Sant'Onofrio, right in front of the pavilion a thought sets me in motion, taking com-mand. It's a force that comes from within, deeper than con-sciousness, than any other part of me. I know where it's taking me, and how determined it is.

I've seen the secretary's room and the hospital director's office a couple of times when I've filled in for the colleague responsible for this area. Nothing showy. The only truly memorable element is a nativity scene behind the large desk. There's also a handsome bookcase, though it pales compared to the painting.

The secretary is a young girl. Now that I'm standing before her, her questioning gaze, there's no more trace of the determination that brought me here. Now all I want to do is run, but it's too late. I have to do something, say something.

"If possible, I'd like to speak to the director." I don't know how much credibility my face inspires. I try, as much as possible, to overcome my anxiety. The secretary doesn't take her eyes off mine. She doesn't move or speak. Two statues facing each other.

"May I ask why?"

The figure before me isn't a secretary, but a guardian; I'll only have a chance to reach the director if I convince her. I try to gather my thoughts.

"I have an idea I'd like to present to him. I work for the cooperative that does the cleaning here, but I'm also an author."

"You can tell me. As soon as he has a moment, I'll speak to him."

Now it's me who can't take my eyes off hers.

"I'd rather talk to him directly. It's a delicate matter."

Silence.

I don't know what to think. A scene plays out in my mind: the secretary starts laughing, louder and louder, any attempt to restrain herself only increases the volume of her laughter. She stares at me, a mixture of pity and disgust in her eyes: "Do you think the director receives all the psychopathic wankers who show up here?" More hellish laughter.

Instead, she opens the huge diary on her desk and starts leafing through it. Tiny handwriting records dozens of appointments marked in pencil, each page equivalent to a nerve-racking, endless day of waiting. The secretary snorts, staring at her diary, then suddenly closes it and, without looking at me, picks up the telephone receiver.

"A young man who works here would like to talk to you."

The secretary hangs up, looks back at me, and unexpectedly smiles.

"You can go in. The director just has a few minutes to spare before his next appointment."

I freeze. I hoped with all my heart to see him, but not immediately. I have to carefully choose my words and maybe rehearse with my mother. Yet here I am, wearing my most threadbare pair of jeans and yesterday's T-shirt.

"I'll go in then."

The secretary laughs.

"Go in, go in."

The director is bent over some papers, scrutinizing them from very close up, no more than four inches away. There are two antique chairs facing his desk, but I remain standing. He slowly raises his head. Here he is.

I've passed him so many times and witnessed so much deference as he walked by. Up close, he has very pale eyes. I'd never noticed.

"So, what can I do for you?"

He does nothing to put me at ease. He conveys an impressive inner rigidity, a hardness he doesn't want to temper with any kind of pleasantry.

"I work in the cooperative that cleans the hospital. I'm also a poet. I've been published in a lot of magazines and anthologies. My first collection is due to come out next year. I have a simple idea. I'd like to propose an anthology of poets who come from the same areas as the children who are treated here. So, all the Mediterranean area, Africa, and Europe, including Russia. A tribute to the hospital in poetry."

There's not a drop of saliva left in my mouth.

The director gives me a long look and studies me inch by inch, musing.

"I love poetry. My first degree was in Literature; I only studied Economics afterwards. Your idea is wonderful, truly, however, as you might imagine, it would be extremely expensive: we would have to invite poets, accommodate them, and give them time to write. One detail in particular makes me somewhat skeptical. I don't know whether you've considered it. Were a poet to come here and merely spend a few days in our hospital, I don't believe they'd be able to give a powerful and sincere account of it. It would be limited to occasional poetry, little more."

I have no answer for the director, simply because I agree with his every word.

"You're right." Disappointment and embarrassment burn across my face.

The director's eyes continue to scrutinize me.

"You told me you're a poet. Why not try writing a book of poems about the hospital?"

I don't know what face I'm making. I haven't written for almost a year, but putting a pen to paper, or pressing a computer key, is merely the final act of writing. This, to precisely define it, is—if anything—a transcription, the gesture that transforms inner workings into shareable symbols. For months now, my head has been exploding with words forced inside by Bambino Gesù, strung together in rhythms, melodies, meters, whatever turns a handful of syllables into a verse. I have no finished poems, but infinite fragments. Pieced together, they form something that I'd previously never really been able to discern but can now see clearly.

The duty to write.

Because I have no other way to bear witness.

"I can try."

The answer couldn't have come out more uncertain.

The director's expression is impassive.

"Very well. We're deliberating over what gift to send our institutional benefactors next Christmas. Perhaps it could be your book. The text will have to be ready by the end of the month so it can be printed by mid-November at the latest."

"I understand."

25

I feel like I'm in the basket of a washing machine, spun around by all the events of the last few weeks.

I was just received by the hospital director to explain my idea. He politely rejected it, then immediately proposed I write a book of poems about the hospital. Me. Me of all people.

If someone—even a couple of hours ago—had recounted this tale, I would've told them that getting sober is possible.

"Nothing doing. He's still on another planet today."

Giovanni proclaims this as soon as he sees me. He's sitting outside the office with Massimo and Luciano. I really can't detach myself from what I've just experienced. My adrenalin has dropped with the passing minutes, but now I'm completely absorbed by the commitment I made to the director. The "I understand" I whispered to him at the end of our meeting echoes in my mind. I should've told him something altogether different, like: "Dear Director, thank you for the opportunity you're giving me, but I have to tell you, for the sake of intellectual honesty, that I think there's only a very remote possibility of me submitting a poetry collection to you by the end of the month, since, as things stand today, October the first, I don't have a single poem."

"I just went to see the director," I tell my teammates under my breath.

"Did you say hello from me?" Giovanni is particularly quick today.

"Could you ask him to do me a favor? Maybe he can give

me one of those apartments they've got for senior doctors, so I don't have to commute anymore." Massimo also can't resist a wisecrack.

"I'm serious, guys."

All three of them give me a long stare.

"Damn, you're getting really good at pranks."

"It's true, I'm telling you. I swear."

"Let's hear it then. What supposedly took you there?"

"I suggested doing an anthology of poets with poems dedicated to the hospital. He said no and asked me to write a book."

My teammates try to laugh about it, then realize, at last, that I'm not joking.

I witness something unexpected. I realize I was incredibly naïve. I would've kept quiet if I'd known. Apart from Massimo, who seemed sincerely happy about the news, Giovanni and Luciano reacted coldly, almost with annoyance. "Look at you, friends with the director now. Congratulations."

Giovanni's quip was intended to wound, and it hit the mark. I don't know why they've taken it this way, but if this is their reaction, I can only imagine how people who can't stand me will respond. I instinctively stop them.

"Now I need to ask you a favor. You've got to swear to God you won't tell anyone about this. Come on, swear."

One by one, albeit unwillingly, they swear.

The shift is spent doing the usual Thursday afternoon chores. A few windows, the HR department asking us to move a filing cabinet glued to the floor by wax, another office—hospital management this time—reporting a bad smell, only to find out later that the stench came from a rotten apple that a worker left in a drawer.

Strangely, the team has been split up this afternoon. We're in the established pairs: me with Massimo; Giovanni with Luciano. We on one side, they on the other. I can't help thinking it was

Giovanni who insisted on this decision. Ever since I told him about the director, he's become inexplicably sullen and refused to look me in the face.

"Give it a few days, Dan. You know what he's like," Massimo told me, noticing my dejection.

It's half four. We walk down the central avenue without a specific destination, like men strolling along a high street to get some fresh air and ogle women. My gaze, wandering beautiful and free, lingers on the window of the hospital's little toy shop.

There's a small notebook with black and white stripes.

It's surrounded by colorful objects, soft toys, games of all shapes and sizes, and an assortment of dolls. Yet it was the only thing I noticed, just as it noticed me.

"Wait a second."

I pay two thousand six hundred lire.

I return to Massimo with the notebook in a paper bag. We resume the walk where we left off.

The team reassembles in the changing room. It's only six o'clock. I've been passively witnessing the games of time since my school days. Everyone wishes for days that aren't too busy, but the hours stretch on shamelessly, never-ending. On the other hand, fortunately, there are days when other people decide, days that are tiring just to think about, so full they end up like gunshots. It goes without saying which are best.

As we smoke, less jocular than usual about what was supposed to be—at least in my head—good news, I pull the notebook out of the paper bag. I run my hand over the black-and-white striped cover. It's slightly rigid. I open it.

The first page is now before me.

It's a clear, unambiguous summons. Both frightening and exhilarating.

It's the whiteness of the page.

It calls, it demands. It's an ultrasound that stirs me from my brain to my bowels. "Has someone got a pen?"

Giovanni takes one from his locker.

I haven't set pen to paper yet.

I know that once I do, I can never go back. Writing commands me like this. I don't have the diary-style approach of those who constantly jot things down. I keep everything inside until the moment of the hemorrhage, the explosion from which everything spills out, word by word.

The first mark is a straight black line. This is followed by squiggles, a sketched silhouette, then another.

I write the first word, the one that's been circling my mind for months now: "Horror." From the little girl on the first day to every other disturbing vision, right up to the nun capable of defeating it.

A blanket of unspeakable sorrows enclosed in a single sound. "Horror."

"Let's go, Dan. It's eight."

I abruptly resurface from the whiteness of the paper.

Another power of writing is its total distortion of time and space. The last two hours only lasted a few minutes.

On the first three or four pages—crossed out and rewritten, still without an ending or a definite opening—is my first poem to the children of Bambino Gesù.

26

Writing exerts a ruthless form of possession.

It's ill-mannered. Rude. It doesn't know day or night. It doesn't care if I'm around people. Its own existence is all that counts, over everything and everyone. Plus, this time I have a deadline that's tight, to put it mildly.

I write non-stop. At home, in the car, at work, then on the reverse journey, from work to home. No moment is spared. Even when I'm not putting pen to paper, I carry on. Even during sleep, words come in dreams, distorted, piled up.

The days have started to rush by, governed by the tempo of the director's deadline.

Today is the eighteenth of October. Monday. Thirteen days to go. Fate has actually given me one more: the thirty-first of October falls on a Sunday. Submission day will be the following Monday, the first of November.

Unintentionally, I've found myself naturally re-organizing my time. There's no point going home when I have to start work again in a few hours. I'm better off staying at the hospital and writing. What I'm sacrificing most of all is the time I should be devoting to sleep, but lying on top of my bed crushed by awkward-sounding verses isn't sleeping anyway.

My teammates have kept my secret.

The three of them are the only ones who know about the burgeoning book. Our relationship has changed. We've gone back to fooling around, constantly joking, though they're not as open with me as before. Perhaps, in their hearts, they see me as an unidentified particle, something ill-defined that could turn against them.

It's Giovanni—more than anyone—who's changed. He hasn't moved on from the moment he heard the news. I've made many attempts to talk to him, to ask him why he's behaving this way. He hides behind his square goatee, saying everything is fine. But he and I know it's not. Luciano has also retreated behind more polite manners and gestures, but in any case our relationship soured long ago, ever since the Saturday night that ended with a near miss and his glasses snapped in two by my unconscious body.

Massimo, on the other hand, has remained pretty much his usual self. He's got to know my rhythms. He's now realized it's useless to talk to me when I've started writing. He asked me several times how I manage to concentrate surrounded by children's sobbing and all kinds of voices and screams. I always gave him the same reply: detaching myself from the outside world isn't so difficult; if anything, it's impossible to marshal what's swirling in my head.

Besides, if you listen carefully, that mass of voices, languages, children's screams, crying, and noises turns out to be something else entirely.

I can only hear it at night, when my teammates go off to the changing room to eat and I'm left writing, sitting by the freshly waxed floors. All these sounds create a single voice with the power of all the lives it encompasses, embraces. It's the hospital's voice. Each time it reveals itself for just a few moments. It doesn't take much to scare it away, to make it return to a mere mass of indistinct sounds and noises.

At home, my mother and father watch everything in utter fear. They could only briefly savor the happiness of seeing their son returned from alcohol to life. Faced with my new state, they're hesitant to take so much as a breath. My mother has repeatedly asked me how I can endure this rhythm, without sleep, barely eating, my little black-and-white-striped notebook beside me even when I sit down for meals. I smile at her hoping to reassure her, but I don't think I can. She, like my father, fears I'll physically collapse and that this collapse will make me reach for the bottle again.

I don't know if this danger exists, though I'm quite certain of another. If I fail to bring the director a good collection of poems, I wouldn't start drinking again. I wouldn't even have the strength for that.

Words can become an obsession, incomprehensible, meaningless sounds. So, you need to stop, look away, do everything you can to forget them.

I've written fifteen poems.

Some have come out of the pen immaculate, intact.

When this happens, you feel blessed by grace, an alignment of the universe enclosed in the sphere of the ballpoint pen.

While some are born ready, others consume hours and hours, days. I've left a couple of them pending. When I reread them, I'm assailed by a deep sense of vertigo, not knowing where to go, how to proceed.

Writing poetry about the children of Bambino Gesù is a completely different trial to those I've faced in the past. My hand isn't free. From the first scribbled word, I've seen thousands of commandments growing around me that I can only answer with blind, total obedience. Everything can be summed up in a single word. Rigor.

Poetry must act as a servant for all the experiences I've had. It must offer itself in its miraculous paucity. Form must be more than mere appearance; it must obey the faces and stories that live through it.

Words are a mystery. They deal with unknown forces. They

can bear the burden of human tension, and they can convey it, fix it on a sheet of paper indefinitely, available through the centuries for those who want to read it. Writers aspire to this strength, this tension. No false beauty. No embellishment will conceal the disfigurement of reality, of children.

I mustn't exist in these poems. Nothing must exist beyond the experiences I'm called to witness. Suffering doesn't stem from words that don't come, but from the kind of natural selection I permit myself to make with regard to what I've seen and experienced. I can't recount everything. It would take me years, perhaps more than a lifetime. I have to sacrifice some of those worlds that have opened up before my eyes. I've asked forgiveness from all of them and I'll continue to do so as long as I live.

Then there's him.
Knock-Knock. Alfredo.
With him I experience something completely new.
I've tried. I try every day.
But it's no use. No words come out.
I can't write about Knock-Knock. A shadow falls when I try. Everything becomes confused, unpronounceable.

27

The best time to shave is at four in the morning. The stubble comes off smoothly, painlessly. A single pass is all it takes for perfect skin.

I don't want to face the director in a sorry state, the way I did a month ago. This time my appearance has to represent me. When I put the manuscript on his desk, I want to be impeccable, as self-assured as possible.

Today is the first of November, Monday.

Submission day.

At five on the dot, I say goodbye to my mother and father. They woke up with me and—apart from private moments in the bathroom—never left my side.

I'd forgotten the size of my father's arms. I practically disappear in his embrace.

"Whatever happens, you did everything you could. You should be proud. Just think how you were a month ago."

Yes. I should be proud. Not for how I am now compared to a month ago, but for having earned his embrace again.

Yet I can't tell myself "whatever happens." It's true I did everything I could, but I can't tolerate the idea of failure. It's easier to imagine myself six feet under.

Not because of the missed opportunity or the poor artistic result; it's not something to do with me and my abilities. What would crush me is an invisible weight, seemingly non-existent, yet alive, huge enough to invade every corner of the world.

I can't fail for their sake.

For all those I wanted to bear witness to through my poetry but couldn't.

They'd chase me all my life, one by one, an army of naked children, harmed by illness, or wearing their best outfit to celebrate their own death. And another army alongside them. Their parents. Distraught, crushed by fatigue without compensation, finally dead too.

Because this is all that remains for a mother and father bereft of a child. They'd give me no respite. Neither here nor in the afterlife.

Autumn only showed up for a week, then retreated, clearing the way for good weather again. As I drive to Rome, I glance at the yellow paper envelope lying on the seat beside me. My collection is in there. When I break a little harder, my right arm responds instinctively, jerking to protect the envelope and its contents. I don't want it to fall forward; the paper could end up crumpled and that's not a good look.

It's ten to six. I enter the hospital with the envelope under my arm. Since last night, from the moment I told myself no more could be done and the collection was complete, an incredible tiredness has set in.

Like everything you don't have, that flails around in your imagination until it becomes far more than it really is, sleep seems so beautiful I could weep. Many long for weeks of holidays in the tropics, or frosty white days spent up and down slopes. I'd just like a week's sleep. Seven days of physical and mental recuperation.

Outside the office, a crowd of colleagues are waiting for six o'clock. There's talk of sending a letter to the cooperative—signed by all of them—to reiterate the demand they made a year ago: cleaning inside a hospital is dangerous for an infinite number of reasons, and those who work here should be paid a risk allowance, as is the case for many workers in other sectors.

The moment they see me, all my colleagues clam up. Fifty eyes look at the yellow paper envelope in my hand.

It's my imagination. No one—aside from my teammates—knows about the book. There's no connection between the fact they've stopped talking and my arrival. Though the doubt lingers.

"The shoes are arriving tomorrow or the day after. I've asked the cooperative for a forty just for you."

Marianna smiles at me; she's never done that before.

I'm not being paranoid. One of my three teammates has talked.

First Giovanni, then Luciano, and finally Massimo.

I give them each a hard stare.

I head off to the changing room.

The green Fiat Bravo is already parked in its spot.

My dismay over this betrayal is immediately dispelled.

The director has arrived.

I change course, briskly entering Sant'Onofrio. I climb the stairs to the director's office two at a time.

It's now a few minutes past six, and naturally there's still no sign of the secretaries. The director has left the door open between the secretary's room and his office. I enter.

He looks a little annoyed when he sees me. I mechanically extend the yellow paper envelope towards him.

"There."

He pulls out the manuscript and tests its weight.

"It's a little slim, wouldn't you say?"

"It's not a very large collection. There are twenty-eight poems in total."

The director fixes his eyes on me.

"Well, poetry can say a great deal in few words. I hope this is true of yours."

"I hope so too."

I leave the office not really knowing what to think. He

seemed disappointed, perhaps he was expecting a book of eighty poems. Or who knows what.

Now I need calm, patience.

I'd give my life to know where to buy them.

"What a bunch of pricks."

I find my colleagues in the changing room, already in uniform. All three look at me blankly.

"Now tell me who talked. Marianna mentioned the shoes, which means she heard something, doesn't it?"

All three remain silent, wearing the same expression. "We didn't say anything, Danny." Massimo speaks first.

"Come on, are you seriously telling me she mentioned the shoes because she suddenly grew a heart?"

"You forget that Marianna knows everyone in here, even the walls. Maybe a secretary talked to someone and asked if they knew that a guy from the cooperative was writing a poetry book. Then they repeated it and within a few days Marianna got wind of it."

Giovanni isn't wrong; his hypothesis is more than possible. After all, the confidentiality about what I was doing lasted until the very last day. I can't complain.

"I hadn't thought of that," I reply.

"Well, there you go. Now to make up for that bullshit, you can get us coffee."

It's the least I can do.

We return to the office, but we already know what the shift has in store for us.

The nun greets us at the door to the ward, stepping aside as soon as she sees us. "Come in, come in." Bouncing up and down, she ushers us in.

The problem recurs cyclically, but no one can do a thing about it. The back of the neuropsychiatric ward, the Ford, is a popular toilet for all sorts of birds, from pigeons and seagulls to ravens and crows. The reason is obvious: the property that adjoins the hospital has a number of trees with foliage overlooking the back of the pavilion. The result is a layer of excrement an inch thick, and it can't have been more than a couple of months since it was last cleaned.

Armed with a hose and broom, we start to melt that blanket of wildly varied colors—from a greenish shade to brown and grey—brushing it all into a corner, then collecting it in black plastic bags. Last time we filled five of them.

I try my hardest not to think about the manuscript and the director. But I can't help myself. Everything worries me, from the final verdict to the time that needs to elapse before I get there. I try to distract myself, but no attempt lasts longer than a few minutes.

Luckily, there's the job at hand, the carpet of excrement we have to remove. If only all work was like this.

At ten-twenty, the back of the Ford is gleaming, magnificent.

The nun emphasizes her emotions with some little standing jumps, just as she did when we came in and when she offered us coffee. She's delighted with our work. "I'll say a prayer for each of you tonight," she said as she waved us out. Then a dark shadow fell over her eyes.

One. Two. Within the space of a few minutes, the birds had already set to work on the new coat of excrement.

The nun pulled a murderous face. She'd bite those birds to death if she could.

The morning continues smoothly.

The playroom windows and entrance. Nothing too heavy or dangerous.

We start with the huge, slanted windows. "Do you remember the last time we cleaned it, Dan? It was one of your first days at work. You looked like a penguin, all quiet. You didn't even know how to hold a wiper."

"Of course," I tell Giovanni. It wasn't one of my first, it was my very first day at work.

Now I'm the one maneuvering the strip on the long telescopic pole. It takes a single gesture to make the window perfect, just as I saw Luciano do many months ago. Inside the playroom—mesmerized by my movements—are a dozen children. At first, they were self-conscious, embarrassed to even look at me. Now they constantly wave at me, pull faces, and jostle to get closer to the windows.

My work is interrupted by the sound of my phone ringing. It's a short number, the kind that doesn't show the last digits of the extension. I recognize that number. It's from the hospital.

"Hello."

"Good morning. When you're ready, the director is waiting for you."

"I'll be right back."

My teammates heard the call, that's all I need to say.

It's eleven-thirty. I handed the manuscript to the director around six this morning.

I'm strangled by angst.

Too little time has passed. It takes longer to even make a basic assessment, unless it's negative.

I climb the stairs to the director's office. I'm drenched in sweat from anxiety, plus my uniform trousers are smeared with bird droppings. The realization that I'm completely unpresentable only adds to my anxiety, which makes me sweat more. A vicious circle.

The secretary doesn't seem in a good mood. Why isn't she in a good mood? But then she smiles, smiles, what a lovely smile she has.

"Go in."

"I'm going."

28

I notice the change as soon as I enter.

The director isn't in his chair behind the desk. He's standing by the window, observing the bustle of people from his vantage point.

He turns towards me.

"Come in, Mencarelli."

I approach, forgetting to breathe the moment I enter. The instant I remember, a hunger for air spreads from my lungs to my nose.

The director—now I'm beside him—begins to stare at me. Up close, his eyes are even more frightening, like a predator's.

"I've worked for this hospital for six years. I'm here every day of the week from six in the morning to late at night."

He looks out the window again.

I'd like to tell him I'm well-aware of his schedule, like everyone who works at Bambino Gesù, but I choose to hold my tongue. I don't want to prolong this wait—finally at an end—in any way. The director remains silently glued to the window. A fair bit of time passes before he finally turns to face me.

"But I've never truly entered it. I only started to become acquainted with it this morning, thanks to you and your poetry."

Then he embraces me, suddenly, incredibly.

I stand motionless. I don't even have the strength to return his gesture. He holds me like this for a few moments. When he breaks away, he smiles at me. I've never seen him do that before, nor embrace anyone for that matter.

"I've already spoken to Tipografie Vaticane, the publisher. They've assured me they'll get to work immediately. By the 20th of this month, we should be ready to go to press. You'll of course be involved in every stage of the process. You can visit them this week to discuss the type of paper and the cover."

"Right."

That's all I say. All my emotion permits. It's not just joy: so many feelings finally have a chance to implode, with no more restraints or delays.

"What's the matter, Mencarelli? Aren't you pleased to hear that?"

The director watches me. Perhaps he expected a more overtly delighted reaction.

"I couldn't be happier. Ever since you suggested I write a collection, I've only lived for this moment. But it's not just my happiness getting in the way. To you, it looks like I'm standing still before you, but I'm actually like a spinning top that's gone berserk. My head is travelling at the speed of light."

"Is it going anywhere nice?"

Memory drags my every cell along the path of these burning, endless months. "It's going through all my memories, every single moment of pain, or wonder. I'd like to see all those who've given me something, one by one, especially those who didn't end up in the poems."

The director takes my arm and squeezes it.

"I sincerely believe they'd all wish to thank you. You portray them very powerfully. I don't suppose it was an easy undertaking."

We both fall silent, watching the bustle down below: a crowd of parents and children in transit, heading for one of the many crossroads in their lives. Many will come out unscathed; others will crash. This morning, right here, for all the thousands of children who'll be restored to freedom and health, a handful will be destined for very different battles fought over their innocent skin. Only a few of that handful—at the end of the war—will emerge victorious.

"It wasn't easy, but there's something that unites me with these people, that allowed me to write. I was also saved by this hospital."

29

On the way back to my teammates, it comes right on cue, whispered in my ears: you could celebrate with a toast, a glass of white, only one, just to add to the merriment.

I don't even respond to evil's invitation. I don't know what it'll come up with in the future, but for now its attempts seem sad, pathetic.

I have to call my mother and father, to tell them it went better than I could've ever imagined.

I'd like to invent a new, wonderful-sounding word, a lexeme containing a thousand feelings, from gratitude to the constant necessity of asking their forgiveness for these past years. But they don't need words; there have always been plenty of those. What my mother and father need is the habit of normality, the return to an existence worth living without having to spend every night on Earth breathless with worry over a son missing God knows where. Yes. I cannot be pardoned through words, however beautiful and accurate they may be, but through the passing of the years, right up to the day—should it ever come—when everything will be a distant memory, painful, but buried.

My teammates are still dealing with the area outside the playroom.

Giovanni and Luciano are tackling the long outdoor linoleum corridor with the scrubber-dryer, while Massimo is cleaning the low windows that partition off the outdoor play area.

They all stop as soon as they see me coming.

No words are needed, not even a gesture.

Just a smile, passed from mouth to mouth.

Giovanni returns to the scrubber-dryer.

"Come on, it's worked out for the poet. The next round of coffee is on him."

Massimo and I have still got to do the playroom's last window.

We pick up where we left off.

As soon as they see me, the children come back to look at me. This time, it doesn't take them nearly as long to overcome their shyness. After no more than a minute, they wrestle to be closest to the window, while on the other side I lather up the long telescopic rod.

When the glass window is finished, invisible in its transparency, we stand looking at each other, they and I, motionless, suddenly serious.

They're inside the hospital, a bunch of sweaty children panting from their frenzied games, beautiful with all the beauty in existence, from every land in the world.

I'm outside, pierced by their gazes, each one nailed in my memory.

"I want to remember everything."

There's no night he doesn't call
with his hard-knuckled voice,
all eyes, an ardent smile,
motionless at his window
he keeps asking for kindness
while years outside pass by
and time strips away what little youth
remains on this aged face,
you know no calendar,
nor anything but being a child,
sick, clinging to his drawings
to soar out of pain,
Knock-Knock, Alfredo one morning
you knocked to enter
and remained inside forever,
continue to make me a house for your gaze,
use me to stay alive in memory.

Acknowledgements

To my family, who lived and endured.

To Davide Rondoni, because friendship is a matter of gestures.

To Francesco Silvano, who entrusted the hospital to my words.

To all the workers who I don't forget.

To Maria Cristina Olati, who edited this debut.

To Carlo Carabba, Marilena Rossi, and all the Mondadori team, who believed in it.

To my wife Piera, who took in a crooked boy and turned him into a man.

To my children, who will one day understand.

To the children of Bambino Gesù Children's Hospital and their parents,
for the blood that unites us,
because I have no other way to bear witness.